Tales and Fantasies

Robert Louis Stevenson

Tales and Fantasies

The present edition is a reproduction of previous publication of this classic work. Minor typographical errors may have been corrected without note; however, for an authentic reading experience the spelling, punctuation, and capitalization have been retained from the original text.

ISBN: 978-1-64799-530-0

CONTENTS

CONTENTS

THE MISADVENTURES OF JOHN NICHOLSON

CHAPTER I

IN WHICH JOHN SOWS THE WIND

John Varey Nicholson was stupid; yet, stupider men than he are now sprawling in Parliament, and lauding themselves as the authors of their own distinction. He was of a fat habit, even from boyhood, and inclined to a cheerful and cursory reading of the face of life; and possibly this attitude of mind was the original cause of his misfortunes. Beyond this hint philosophy is silent on his career, and superstition steps in with the more ready explanation that he was detested of the gods.

His father—that iron gentleman—had long ago enthroned himself on the heights of the Disruption Principles. What these are (and in spite of their grim name they are quite innocent) no array of terms would render thinkable to the merely English intelligence; but to the Scot they often prove unctuously nourishing, and Mr. Nicholson found in them the milk of lions. About the period when the churches convene at Edinburgh in their annual assemblies, he was to be seen descending the Mound in the company of divers redheaded clergymen: these voluble, he only contributing oracular nods, brief negatives, and the austere spectacle of his stretched upper lip. The names of Candlish and Begg were frequent in these interviews, and occasionally the talk ran on the Residuary Establishment and the doings of one Lee. A stranger to the tight little theological kingdom of Scotland might have listened and gathered literally nothing. And Mr. Nicholson (who was not a dull man) knew this, and raged at it. He knew there was a vast world outside, to whom Disruption Principles were as the chatter of tree-

1

top apes; the paper brought him chill whiffs from it; he had met Englishmen who had asked lightly if he did not belong to the Church of Scotland, and then had failed to be much interested by his elucidation of that nice point; it was an evil, wild, rebellious world, lying sunk in dozenedness, for nothing short of a Scots word will paint this Scotsman's feelings. And when he entered into his own house in Randolph Crescent (south side), and shut the door behind him, his heart swelled with security. Here, at least, was a citadel impregnable by right-hand defections or left-hand extremes. Here was a family where prayers came at the same hour, where the Sabbath literature was unimpeachably selected, where the guest who should have leaned to any false opinion was instantly set down, and over which there reigned all week, and grew denser on Sundays, a silence that was agreeable to his ear, and a gloom that he found comfortable.

Mrs. Nicholson had died about thirty, and left him with three children: a daughter two years, and a son about eight years younger than John; and John himself, the unlucky bearer of a name infamous in English history. The daughter, Maria, was a good girl—dutiful, pious, dull, but so easily startled that to speak to her was quite a perilous enterprise. 'I don't think I care to talk about that, if you please,' she would say, and strike the boldest speechless by her unmistakable pain; this upon all topics—dress, pleasure, morality, politics, in which the formula was changed to 'my papa thinks otherwise,' and even religion, unless it was approached with a particular whining tone of voice. Alexander, the younger brother, was sickly, clever, fond of books and drawing, and full of satirical remarks. In the midst of these, imagine that natural, clumsy, unintelligent, and mirthful animal, John; mighty well-behaved in comparison with other lads, although not up to the mark of the house in Randolph Crescent; full of a sort of blundering affection, full of caresses, which were never very warmly received; full of sudden and loud laughter which rang out in that still house like curses. Mr. Nicholson himself had a great fund of humour, of the Scots order—intellectual, turning on the observation of men; his own character, for instance—if he could have seen it in another—would have been a rare feast to him; but his son's empty guffaws over a broken plate, and empty, almost light-hearted remarks, struck him with pain as the indices of a weak mind.

Outside the family John had early attached himself (much as a dog may follow a marquis) to the steps of Alan Houston, a lad about a year older than himself, idle, a trifle wild, the heir to a good estate

2

which was still in the hands of a rigorous trustee, and so royally content with himself that he took John's devotion as a thing of course. The intimacy was gall to Mr. Nicholson; it took his son from the house, and he was a jealous parent; it kept him from the office, and he was a martinet; lastly, Mr. Nicholson was ambitious for his family (in which, and the Disruption Principles, he entirely lived), and he hated to see a son of his play second fiddle to an idler. After some hesitation, he ordered that the friendship should cease—an unfair command, though seemingly inspired by the spirit of prophecy; and John, saying nothing, continued to disobey the order under the rose.

John was nearly nineteen when he was one day dismissed rather earlier than usual from his father's office, where he was studying the practice of the law. It was Saturday; and except that he had a matter of four hundred pounds in his pocket which it was his duty to hand over to the British Linen Company's Bank, he had the whole afternoon at his disposal. He went by Princes Street enjoying the mild sunshine, and the little thrill of easterly wind that tossed the flags along that terrace of palaces, and tumbled the green trees in the garden. The band was playing down in the valley under the castle; and when it came to the turn of the pipers, he heard their wild sounds with a stirring of the blood. Something distantly martial woke in him; and he thought of Miss Mackenzie, whom he was to meet that day at dinner.

Now, it is undeniable that he should have gone directly to the bank, but right in the way stood the billiard-room of the hotel where Alan was almost certain to be found; and the temptation proved too strong. He entered the billiard-room, and was instantly greeted by his friend, cue in hand.

'Nicholson,' said he, 'I want you to lend me a pound or two till Monday.'

'You've come to the right shop, haven't you?' returned John. 'I have twopence.'

'Nonsense,' said Alan. 'You can get some. Go and borrow at your tailor's; they all do it. Or I'll tell you what: pop your watch.'

'Oh, yes, I dare say,' said John. 'And how about my father?'

'How is he to know? He doesn't wind it up for you at night, does he?' inquired Alan, at which John guffawed. 'No, seriously; I am in

3

a fix,' continued the tempter. 'I have lost some money to a man here. I'll give it you to-night, and you can get the heir-loom out again on Monday. Come; it's a small service, after all. I would do a good deal more for you.'

Whereupon John went forth, and pawned his gold watch under the assumed name of John Froggs, 85 Pleasance. But the nervousness that assailed him at the door of that inglorious haunt—a pawnshop—and the effort necessary to invent the pseudonym (which, somehow, seemed to him a necessary part of the procedure), had taken more time than he imagined: and when he returned to the billiard-room with the spoils, the bank had already closed its doors.

This was a shrewd knock. 'A piece of business had been neglected.' He heard these words in his father's trenchant voice, and trembled, and then dodged the thought. After all, who was to know? He must carry four hundred pounds about with him till Monday, when the neglect could be surreptitiously repaired; and meanwhile, he was free to pass the afternoon on the encircling divan of the billiard-room, smoking his pipe, sipping a pint of ale, and enjoying to the masthead the modest pleasures of admiration.

None can admire like a young man. Of all youth's passions and pleasures, this is the most common and least alloyed; and every flash of Alan's black eyes; every aspect of his curly head; every graceful reach, every easy, stand-off attitude of waiting; ay, and down to his shirt-sleeves and wrist-links, were seen by John through a luxurious glory. He valued himself by the possession of that royal friend, hugged himself upon the thought, and swam in warm azure; his own defects, like vanquished difficulties, becoming things on which to plume himself. Only when he thought of Miss Mackenzie there fell upon his mind a shadow of regret; that young lady was worthy of better things than plain John Nicholson, still known among schoolmates by the derisive name of 'Fatty'; and he felt, if he could chalk a cue, or stand at ease, with such a careless grace as Alan, he could approach the object of his sentiments with a less crushing sense of inferiority.

Before they parted, Alan made a proposal that was startling in the extreme. He would be at Colette's that night about twelve, he said. Why should not John come there and get the money? To go to Colette's was to see life, indeed; it was wrong; it was against the laws; it partook, in a very dingy manner, of adventure. Were it

4

known, it was the sort of exploit that disconsidered a young man for good with the more serious classes, but gave him a standing with the riotous. And yet Colette's was not a hell; it could not come, without vaulting hyperbole, under the rubric of a gilded saloon; and, if it was a sin to go there, the sin was merely local and municipal. Colette (whose name I do not know how to spell, for I was never in epistolary communication with that hospitable outlaw) was simply an unlicensed publican, who gave suppers after eleven at night, the Edinburgh hour of closing. If you belonged to a club, you could get a much better supper at the same hour, and lose not a jot in public esteem. But if you lacked that qualification, and were an hungered, or inclined toward conviviality at unlawful hours, Colette's was your only port. You were very ill-supplied. The company was not recruited from the Senate or the Church, though the Bar was very well represented on the only occasion on which I flew in the face of my country's laws, and, taking my reputation in my hand, penetrated into that grim supper-house. And Colette's frequenters, thrillingly conscious of wrong-doing and 'that two-handed engine (the policeman) at the door,' were perhaps inclined to somewhat feverish excess. But the place was in no sense a very bad one; and it is somewhat strange to me, at this distance of time, how it had acquired its dangerous repute.

In precisely the same spirit as a man may debate a project to ascend the Matterhorn or to cross Africa, John considered Alan's proposal, and, greatly daring, accepted it. As he walked home, the thoughts of this excursion out of the safe places of life into the wild and arduous, stirred and struggled in his imagination with the image of Miss Mackenzie—incongruous and yet kindred thoughts, for did not each imply unusual tightening of the pegs of resolution? did not each woo him forth and warn him back again into himself?

Between these two considerations, at least, he was more than usually moved; and when he got to Randolph Crescent, he quite forgot the four hundred pounds in the inner pocket of his greatcoat, hung up the coat, with its rich freight, upon his particular pin of the hatstand; and in the very action sealed his doom.

CHAPTER II

IN WHICH JOHN REAPS THE WHIRLWIND

About half-past ten it was John's brave good fortune to offer his arm to Miss Mackenzie, and escort her home. The night was chill and starry; all the way eastward the trees of the different gardens rustled and looked black. Up the stone gully of Leith Walk, when they came to cross it, the breeze made a rush and set the flames of the street-lamps quavering; and when at last they had mounted to the Royal Terrace, where Captain Mackenzie lived, a great salt freshness came in their faces from the sea. These phases of the walk remained written on John's memory, each emphasised by the touch of that light hand on his arm; and behind all these aspects of the nocturnal city he saw, in his mind's-eye, a picture of the lighted drawing-room at home where he had sat talking with Flora; and his father, from the other end, had looked on with a kind and ironical smile. John had read the significance of that smile, which might have escaped a stranger. Mr. Nicholson had remarked his son's entanglement with satisfaction, tinged by humour; and his smile, if it still was a thought contemptuous, had implied consent.

At the captain's door the girl held out her hand, with a certain emphasis; and John took it and kept it a little longer, and said, 'Good-night, Flora, dear,' and was instantly thrown into much fear by his presumption. But she only laughed, ran up the steps, and rang the bell; and while she was waiting for the door to open, kept close in the porch, and talked to him from that point as out of a fortification. She had a knitted shawl over her head; her blue Highland eyes took the light from the neighbouring street-lamp and sparkled; and when the door opened and closed upon her, John felt cruelly alone.

He proceeded slowly back along the terrace in a tender glow; and when he came to Greenside Church, he halted in a doubtful mind. Over the crown of the Calton Hill, to his left, lay the way to Colette's, where Alan would soon be looking for his arrival, and where he would now have no more consented to go than he would have wilfully wallowed in a bog; the touch of the girl's hand on his sleeve,

6

and the kindly light in his father's eyes, both loudly forbidding. But right before him was the way home, which pointed only to bed, a place of little ease for one whose fancy was strung to the lyrical pitch, and whose not very ardent heart was just then tumultuously moved. The hilltop, the cool air of the night, the company of the great monuments, the sight of the city under his feet, with its hills and valleys and crossing files of lamps, drew him by all he had of the poetic, and he turned that way; and by that quite innocent deflection, ripened the crop of his venial errors for the sickle of destiny.

On a seat on the hill above Greenside he sat for perhaps half an hour, looking down upon the lamps of Edinburgh, and up at the lamps of heaven. Wonderful were the resolves he formed; beautiful and kindly were the vistas of future life that sped before him. He uttered to himself the name of Flora in so many touching and dramatic keys, that he became at length fairly melted with tenderness, and could have sung aloud. At that juncture a certain creasing in his greatcoat caught his ear. He put his hand into his pocket, pulled forth the envelope that held the money, and sat stupefied. The Calton Hill, about this period, had an ill name of nights; and to be sitting there with four hundred pounds that did not belong to him was hardly wise. He looked up. There was a man in a very bad hat a little on one side of him, apparently looking at the scenery; from a little on the other a second night-walker was drawing very quietly near. Up jumped John. The envelope fell from his hands; he stooped to get it, and at the same moment both men ran in and closed with him.

A little after, he got to his feet very sore and shaken, the poorer by a purse which contained exactly one penny postage-stamp, by a cambric handkerchief, and by the all-important envelope.

Here was a young man on whom, at the highest point of lovely exaltation, there had fallen a blow too sharp to be supported alone; and not many hundred yards away his greatest friend was sitting at supper—ay, and even expecting him. Was it not in the nature of man that he should run there? He went in quest of sympathy—in quest of that droll article that we all suppose ourselves to want when in a strait, and have agreed to call advice; and he went, besides, with vague but rather splendid expectations of relief. Alan was rich, or would be so when he came of age. By a stroke of the pen he might remedy this misfortune, and avert that dreaded interview with Mr.

Nicholson, from which John now shrunk in imagination as the hand draws back from fire.

Close under the Calton Hill there runs a certain narrow avenue, part street, part by-road. The head of it faces the doors of the prison; its tail descends into the sunless slums of the Low Calton. On one hand it is overhung by the crags of the hill, on the other by an old graveyard. Between these two the roadway runs in a trench, sparsely lighted at night, sparsely frequented by day, and bordered, when it was cleared the place of tombs, by dingy and ambiguous houses. One of these was the house of Colette; and at his door our ill-starred John was presently beating for admittance. In an evil hour he satisfied the jealous inquiries of the contraband hotel-keeper; in an evil hour he penetrated into the somewhat unsavoury interior. Alan, to be sure, was there, seated in a room lighted by noisy gas-jets, beside a dirty table-cloth, engaged on a coarse meal, and in the company of several tipsy members of the junior bar. But Alan was not sober; he had lost a thousand pounds upon a horse-race, had received the news at dinner-time, and was now, in default of any possible means of extrication, drowning the memory of his predicament. He to help John! The thing was impossible; he couldn't help himself.

'If you have a beast of a father,' said he, 'I can tell you I have a brute of a trustee.'

'I'm not going to hear my father called a beast,' said John with a beating heart, feeling that he risked the last sound rivet of the chain that bound him to life.

But Alan was quite good-natured.

'All right, old fellow,' said he. 'Mos' respec'able man your father.' And he introduced his friend to his companions as 'old Nicholson the what-d'ye-call-um's son.'

John sat in dumb agony. Colette's foul walls and maculate table-linen, and even down to Colette's villainous casters, seemed like objects in a nightmare. And just then there came a knock and a scurrying; the police, so lamentably absent from the Calton Hill, appeared upon the scene; and the party, taken flagrante delicto, with their glasses at their elbow, were seized, marched up to the police office, and all duly summoned to appear as witnesses in the consequent case against that arch-shebeener, Colette.

8

It was a sorrowful and a mightily sobered company that came forth again. The vague terror of public opinion weighed generally on them all; but there were private and particular horrors on the minds of individuals. Alan stood in dread of his trustee, already sorely tried. One of the group was the son of a country minister, another of a judge; John, the unhappiest of all, had David Nicholson to father, the idea of facing whom on such a scandalous subject was physically sickening. They stood awhile consulting under the buttresses of Saint Giles; thence they adjourned to the lodgings of one of the number in North Castle Street, where (for that matter) they might have had quite as good a supper, and far better drink, than in the dangerous paradise from which they had been routed. There, over an almost tearful glass, they debated their position. Each explained he had the world to lose if the affair went on, and he appeared as a witness. It was remarkable what bright prospects were just then in the very act of opening before each of that little company of youths, and what pious consideration for the feelings of their families began now to well from them. Each, moreover, was in an odd state of destitution. Not one could bear his share of the fine; not one but evinced a wonderful twinkle of hope that each of the others (in succession) was the very man who could step in to make good the deficit. One took a high hand; he could not pay his share; if it went to a trial, he should bolt; he had always felt the English Bar to be his true sphere. Another branched out into touching details about his family, and was not listened to. John, in the midst of this disorderly competition of poverty and meanness, sat stunned, contemplating the mountain bulk of his misfortunes.

At last, upon a pledge that each should apply to his family with a common frankness, this convention of unhappy young asses broke up, went down the common stair, and in the grey of the spring morning, with the streets lying dead empty all about them, the lamps burning on into the daylight in diminished lustre, and the birds beginning to sound premonitory notes from the groves of the town gardens, went each his own way with bowed head and echoing footfall.

The rooks were awake in Randolph Crescent; but the windows looked down, discreetly blinded, on the return of the prodigal. John's pass-key was a recent privilege; this was the first time it had been used; and, oh! with what a sickening sense of his unworthiness he now inserted it into the well-oiled lock and entered that citadel of the proprieties! All slept; the gas in the hall had been left faintly burning to light his return; a dreadful stillness reigned, broken by the deep ticking of the eight-day clock. He put the gas out, and sat on a chair in the hall, waiting and counting the minutes, longing for any human countenance. But when at last he heard the alarm spring its rattle in the lower story, and the servants begin to be about, he instantly lost heart, and fled to his own room, where he threw himself upon the bed.

CHAPTER III

IN WHICH JOHN ENJOYS THE HARVEST HOME

Shortly after breakfast, at which he assisted with a highly tragical countenance, John sought his father where he sat, presumably in religious meditation, on the Sabbath mornings. The old gentleman looked up with that sour, inquisitive expression that came so near to smiling and was so different in effect.

'This is a time when I do not like to be disturbed,' he said.

'I know that,' returned John; 'but I have—I want—I've made a dreadful mess of it,' he broke out, and turned to the window.

Mr. Nicholson sat silent for an appreciable time, while his unhappy son surveyed the poles in the back green, and a certain yellow cat that was perched upon the wall. Despair sat upon John as he gazed; and he raged to think of the dreadful series of his misdeeds, and the essential innocence that lay behind them.

'Well,' said the father, with an obvious effort, but in very quiet tones, 'what is it?'

'Maclean gave me four hundred pounds to put in the bank, sir,' began John; 'and I'm sorry to say that I've been robbed of it!'

'Robbed of it?' cried Mr. Nicholson, with a strong rising inflection. 'Robbed? Be careful what you say, John!'

'I can't say anything else, sir; I was just robbed of it,' said John, in desperation, sullenly.

'And where and when did this extraordinary event take place?' inquired the father.

'On the Calton Hill about twelve last night.'

'The Calton Hill?' repeated Mr. Nicholson. 'And what were you doing there at such a time of the night?'

11

'Nothing, sir,' says John.

Mr. Nicholson drew in his breath.

'And how came the money in your hands at twelve last night?' he asked, sharply.

'I neglected that piece of business,' said John, anticipating comment; and then in his own dialect: 'I clean forgot all about it.'

'Well,' said his father, 'it's a most extraordinary story. Have you communicated with the police?'

'I have,' answered poor John, the blood leaping to his face. 'They think they know the men that did it. I dare say the money will be recovered, if that was all,' said he, with a desperate indifference, which his father set down to levity; but which sprung from the consciousness of worse behind.

'Your mother's watch, too?' asked Mr. Nicholson.

'Oh, the watch is all right!' cried John. 'At least, I mean I was coming to the watch—the fact is, I am ashamed to say, I—I had pawned the watch before. Here is the ticket; they didn't find that; the watch can be redeemed; they don't sell pledges.' The lad panted out these phrases, one after another, like minute guns; but at the last word, which rang in that stately chamber like an oath, his heart failed him utterly; and the dreaded silence settled on father and son.

It was broken by Mr. Nicholson picking up the pawn-ticket: 'John Froggs, 85 Pleasance,' he read; and then turning upon John, with a brief flash of passion and disgust, 'Who is John Froggs?' he cried.

'Nobody,' said John. 'It was just a name.'

'An alias,' his father commented.

'Oh! I think scarcely quite that,' said the culprit; 'it's a form, they all do it, the man seemed to understand, we had a great deal of fun over the name—'

He paused at that, for he saw his father wince at the picture like a man physically struck; and again there was silence.

'I do not think,' said Mr. Nicholson, at last, 'that I am an ungenerous father. I have never grudged you money within reason, for any

12

avowable purpose; you had just to come to me and speak. And now I find that you have forgotten all decency and all natural feeling, and actually pawned—pawned—your mother's watch. You must have had some temptation; I will do you the justice to suppose it was a strong one. What did you want with this money?'

'I would rather not tell you, sir,' said John. 'It will only make you angry.'

'I will not be fenced with,' cried his father. 'There must be an end of disingenuous answers. What did you want with this money?'

'To lend it to Houston, sir,' says John.

'I thought I had forbidden you to speak to that young man?' asked the father.

'Yes, sir,' said John; 'but I only met him.'

'Where?' came the deadly question.

And 'In a billiard-room' was the damning answer. Thus, had John's single departure from the truth brought instant punishment. For no other purpose but to see Alan would he have entered a billiard-room; but he had desired to palliate the fact of his disobedience, and now it appeared that he frequented these disreputable haunts upon his own account.

Once more Mr. Nicholson digested the vile tidings in silence, and when John stole a glance at his father's countenance, he was abashed to see the marks of suffering.

'Well,' said the old gentleman, at last, 'I cannot pretend not to be simply bowed down. I rose this morning what the world calls a happy man—happy, at least, in a son of whom I thought I could be reasonably proud—'

But it was beyond human nature to endure this longer, and John interrupted almost with a scream. 'Oh, wheest!' he cried, 'that's not all, that's not the worst of it—it's nothing! How could I tell you were proud of me? Oh! I wish, I wish that I had known; but you always said I was such a disgrace! And the dreadful thing is this: we were all taken up last night, and we have to pay Colette's fine among the six, or we'll be had up for evidence—shebeening it is. They made me swear to tell you; but for my part,' he cried, bursting into tears, 'I

13

just wish that I was dead!' And he fell on his knees before a chair and hid his face.

Whether his father spoke, or whether he remained long in the room or at once departed, are points lost to history. A horrid turmoil of mind and body; bursting sobs; broken, vanishing thoughts, now of indignation, now of remorse; broken elementary whiffs of consciousness, of the smell of the horse-hair on the chair bottom, of the jangling of church bells that now began to make day horrible throughout the confines of the city, of the hard floor that bruised his knees, of the taste of tears that found their way into his mouth: for a period of time, the duration of which I cannot guess, while I refuse to dwell longer on its agony, these were the whole of God's world for John Nicholson.

When at last, as by the touching of a spring, he returned again to clearness of consciousness and even a measure of composure, the bells had but just done ringing, and the Sabbath silence was still marred by the patter of belated feet. By the clock above the fire, as well as by these more speaking signs, the service had not long begun; and the unhappy sinner, if his father had really gone to church, might count on near two hours of only comparative unhappiness. With his father, the superlative degree returned infallibly. He knew it by every shrinking fibre in his body, he knew it by the sudden dizzy whirling of his brain, at the mere thought of that calamity. An hour and a half, perhaps an hour and three-quarters, if the doctor was long-winded, and then would begin again that active agony from which, even in the dull ache of the present, he shrunk as from the bite of fire. He saw, in a vision, the family pew, the somnolent cushions, the Bibles, the psalm-books, Maria with her smelling-salts, his father sitting spectacled and critical; and at once he was struck with indignation, not unjustly. It was inhuman to go off to church, and leave a sinner in suspense, unpunished, unforgiven. And at the very touch of criticism, the paternal sanctity was lessened; yet the paternal terror only grew; and the two strands of feeling pushed him in the same direction.

And suddenly there came upon him a mad fear lest his father should have locked him in. The notion had no ground in sense; it was probably no more than a reminiscence of similar calamities in childhood, for his father's room had always been the chamber of inquisition and the scene of punishment; but it stuck so rigorously in his mind that he must instantly approach the door and prove its untruth. As he went, he struck upon a drawer left open in the

14

business table. It was the money-drawer, a measure of his father's disarray: the money-drawer—perhaps a pointing providence! Who is to decide, when even divines differ between a providence and a temptation? or who, sitting calmly under his own vine, is to pass a judgment on the doings of a poor, hunted dog, slavishly afraid, slavishly rebellious, like John Nicholson on that particular Sunday? His hand was in the drawer, almost before his mind had conceived the hope; and rising to his new situation, he wrote, sitting in his father's chair and using his father's blotting-pad, his pitiful apology and farewell:—

'My dear Father,—I have taken the money, but I will pay it back as soon as I am able. You will never hear of me again. I did not mean any harm by anything, so I hope you will try and forgive me. I wish you would say good-bye to Alexander and Maria, but not if you don't want to. I could not wait to see you, really. Please try to forgive me. Your affectionate son,

John Nicholson.'

The coins abstracted and the missive written, he could not be gone too soon from the scene of these transgressions; and remembering how his father had once returned from church, on some slight illness, in the middle of the second psalm, he durst not even make a packet of a change of clothes. Attired as he was, he slipped from the paternal doors, and found himself in the cool spring air, the thin spring sunshine, and the great Sabbath quiet of the city, which was now only pointed by the cawing of the rooks. There was not a soul in Randolph Crescent, nor a soul in Queensferry Street; in this outdoor privacy and the sense of escape, John took heart again; and with a pathetic sense of leave-taking, he even ventured up the lane and stood awhile, a strange peri at the gates of a quaint paradise, by the west end of St. George's Church. They were singing within; and by a strange chance, the tune was 'St. George's, Edinburgh,' which bears the name, and was first sung in the choir of that church. 'Who is this King of Glory?' went the voices from within; and, to John, this was like the end of all Christian observances, for he was now to be a wild man like Ishmael, and his life was to be cast in homeless places and with godless people.

It was thus, with no rising sense of the adventurous, but in mere desolation and despair, that he turned his back on his native city, and set out on foot for California, with a more immediate eye to Glasgow.

CHAPTER IV

THE SECOND SOWING

It is no part of mine to narrate the adventures of John Nicholson, which were many, but simply his more momentous misadventures, which were more than he desired, and, by human standards, more than he deserved; how he reached California, how he was rooked, and robbed, and beaten, and starved; how he was at last taken up by charitable folk, restored to some degree of self-complacency, and installed as a clerk in a bank in San Francisco, it would take too long to tell; nor in these episodes were there any marks of the peculiar Nicholsonic destiny, for they were just such matters as befell some thousands of other young adventurers in the same days and places. But once posted in the bank, he fell for a time into a high degree of good fortune, which, as it was only a longer way about to fresh disaster, it behooves me to explain.

It was his luck to meet a young man in what is technically called a 'dive,' and thanks to his monthly wages, to extricate this new acquaintance from a position of present disgrace and possible danger in the future. This young man was the nephew of one of the Nob Hill magnates, who run the San Francisco Stock Exchange, much as more humble adventurers, in the corner of some public park at home, may be seen to perform the simple artifice of pea and thimble: for their own profit, that is to say, and the discouragement of public gambling. It was thus in his power—and, as he was of grateful temper, it was among the things that he desired—to put John in the way of growing rich; and thus, without thought or industry, or so much as even understanding the game at which he played, but by simply buying and selling what he was told to buy and sell, that plaything of fortune was presently at the head of between eleven and twelve thousand pounds, or, as he reckoned it, of upward of sixty thousand dollars.

How he had come to deserve this wealth, any more than how he had formerly earned disgrace at home, was a problem beyond the reach of his philosophy. It was true that he had been industrious at the bank, but no more so than the cashier, who had seven small children and was visibly sinking in decline. Nor was the step which

16

had determined his advance—a visit to a dive with a month's wages in his pocket—an act of such transcendent virtue, or even wisdom, as to seem to merit the favour of the gods. From some sense of this, and of the dizzy see-saw—heaven-high, hell-deep—on which men sit clutching; or perhaps fearing that the sources of his fortune might be insidiously traced to some root in the field of petty cash; he stuck to his work, said not a word of his new circumstances, and kept his account with a bank in a different quarter of the town. The concealment, innocent as it seems, was the first step in the second tragicomedy of John's existence.

Meanwhile, he had never written home. Whether from diffidence or shame, or a touch of anger, or mere procrastination, or because (as we have seen) he had no skill in literary arts, or because (as I am sometimes tempted to suppose) there is a law in human nature that prevents young men—not otherwise beasts—from the performance of this simple act of piety—months and years had gone by, and John had never written. The habit of not writing, indeed, was already fixed before he had begun to come into his fortune; and it was only the difficulty of breaking this long silence that withheld him from an instant restitution of the money he had stolen or (as he preferred to call it) borrowed. In vain he sat before paper, attending on inspiration; that heavenly nymph, beyond suggesting the words 'my dear father,' remained obstinately silent; and presently John would crumple up the sheet and decide, as soon as he had 'a good chance,' to carry the money home in person. And this delay, which is indefensible, was his second step into the snares of fortune.

Ten years had passed, and John was drawing near to thirty. He had kept the promise of his boyhood, and was now of a lusty frame, verging toward corpulence; good features, good eyes, a genial manner, a ready laugh, a long pair of sandy whiskers, a dash of an American accent, a close familiarity with the great American joke, and a certain likeness to a R-y-l P-rs-n-ge, who shall remain nameless for me, made up the man's externals as he could be viewed in society. Inwardly, in spite of his gross body and highly masculine whiskers, he was more like a maiden lady than a man of twenty-nine.

It chanced one day, as he was strolling down Market Street on the eve of his fortnight's holiday, that his eye was caught by certain railway bills, and in very idleness of mind he calculated that he might be home for Christmas if he started on the morrow. The fancy thrilled him with desire, and in one moment he decided he would go.

There was much to be done: his portmanteau to be packed, a credit to be got from the bank where he was a wealthy customer, and certain offices to be transacted for that other bank in which he was an humble clerk; and it chanced, in conformity with human nature, that out of all this business it was the last that came to be neglected. Night found him, not only equipped with money of his own, but once more (as on that former occasion) saddled with a considerable sum of other people's.

Now it chanced there lived in the same boarding-house a fellow-clerk of his, an honest fellow, with what is called a weakness for drink—though it might, in this case, have been called a strength, for the victim had been drunk for weeks together without the briefest intermission. To this unfortunate John intrusted a letter with an inclosure of bonds, addressed to the bank manager. Even as he did so he thought he perceived a certain haziness of eye and speech in his trustee; but he was too hopeful to be stayed, silenced the voice of warning in his bosom, and with one and the same gesture committed the money to the clerk, and himself into the hands of destiny.

I dwell, even at the risk of tedium, on John's minutest errors, his case being so perplexing to the moralist; but we have done with them now, the roll is closed, the reader has the worst of our poor hero, and I leave him to judge for himself whether he or John has been the less deserving. Henceforth we have to follow the spectacle of a man who was a mere whip-top for calamity; on whose unmerited misadventures not even the humourist can look without pity, and not even the philosopher without alarm.

That same night the clerk entered upon a bout of drunkenness so consistent as to surprise even his intimate acquaintance. He was speedily ejected from the boarding-house; deposited his portmanteau with a perfect stranger, who did not even catch his name; wandered he knew not where, and was at last hove-to, all standing, in a hospital at Sacramento. There, under the impenetrable alias of the number of his bed, the crapulous being lay for some more days unconscious of all things, and of one thing in particular: that the police were after him. Two months had come and gone before the convalescent in the Sacramento hospital was identified with Kirkman, the absconding San Francisco clerk; even then, there must elapse nearly a fortnight more till the perfect

18

stranger could be hunted up, the portmanteau recovered, and John's letter carried at length to its destination, the seal still unbroken, the inclosure still intact.

Meanwhile, John had gone upon his holidays without a word, which was irregular; and there had disappeared with him a certain sum of money, which was out of all bounds of palliation. But he was known to be careless, and believed to be honest; the manager besides had a regard for him; and little was said, although something was no doubt thought, until the fortnight was finally at an end, and the time had come for John to reappear. Then, indeed, the affair began to look black; and when inquiries were made, and the penniless clerk was found to have amassed thousands of dollars, and kept them secretly in a rival establishment, the stoutest of his friends abandoned him, the books were overhauled for traces of ancient and artful fraud, and though none were found, there still prevailed a general impression of loss. The telegraph was set in motion; and the correspondent of the bank in Edinburgh, for which place it was understood that John had armed himself with extensive credits, was warned to communicate with the police.

Now this correspondent was a friend of Mr. Nicholson's; he was well acquainted with the tale of John's calamitous disappearance from Edinburgh; and putting one thing with another, hasted with the first word of this scandal, not to the police, but to his friend. The old gentleman had long regarded his son as one dead; John's place had been taken, the memory of his faults had already fallen to be one of those old aches, which awaken again indeed upon occasion, but which we can always vanquish by an effort of the will; and to have the long lost resuscitated in a fresh disgrace was doubly bitter.

'Macewen,' said the old man, 'this must be hushed up, if possible. If I give you a cheek for this sum, about which they are certain, could you take it on yourself to let the matter rest?'

'I will,' said Macewen. 'I will take the risk of it.'

'You understand,' resumed Mr. Nicholson, speaking precisely, but with ashen lips, 'I do this for my family, not for that unhappy young man. If it should turn out that these suspicions are correct, and he has embezzled large sums, he must lie on his bed as he has made it.' And then looking up at Macewen with a nod, and one of his strange smiles: 'Good-bye,' said he, and Macewen, perceiving the case to be too grave for consolation, took himself off, and blessed God on his way home that he was childless.

19

CHAPTER V

THE PRODIGAL'S RETURN

By a little after noon on the eve of Christmas, John had left his portmanteau in the cloak-room, and stepped forth into Princes Street with a wonderful expansion of the soul, such as men enjoy on the completion of long-nourished schemes. He was at home again, incognito and rich; presently he could enter his father's house by means of the pass-key, which he had piously preserved through all his wanderings; he would throw down the borrowed money; there would be a reconciliation, the details of which he frequently arranged; and he saw himself, during the next month, made welcome in many stately houses at many frigid dinner-parties, taking his share in the conversation with the freedom of the man and the traveller, and laying down the law upon finance with the authority of the successful investor. But this programme was not to be begun before evening—not till just before dinner, indeed, at which meal the reassembled family were to sit roseate, and the best wine, the modern fatted calf, should flow for the prodigal's return.

Meanwhile he walked familiar streets, merry reminiscences crowding round him, sad ones also, both with the same surprising pathos. The keen frosty air; the low, rosy, wintry sun; the castle, hailing him like an old acquaintance; the names of friends on door-plates; the sight of friends whom he seemed to recognise, and whom he eagerly avoided, in the streets; the pleasant chant of the north-country accent; the dome of St. George's reminding him of his last penitential moments in the lane, and of that King of Glory whose name had echoed ever since in the saddest corner of his memory; and the gutters where he had learned to slide, and the shop where he had bought his skates, and the stones on which he had trod, and the railings in which he had rattled his clachan as he went to school; and all those thousand and one nameless particulars, which the eye sees without noting, which the memory keeps indeed yet without knowing, and which, taken one with another, build up for us the aspect of the place that we call home: all these besieged him, as he went, with both delight and sadness.

His first visit was for Houston, who had a house on Regent Terrace, kept for him in old days by an aunt. The door was opened (to his surprise) upon the chain, and a voice asked him from within what he wanted.

'I want Mr. Houston—Mr. Alan Houston,' said he.

'And who are ye?' said the voice.

'This is most extraordinary,' thought John; and then aloud he told his name.

'No' young Mr. John?' cried the voice, with a sudden increase of Scotch accent, testifying to a friendlier feeling.

'The very same,' said John.

And the old butler removed his defences, remarking only 'I thocht ye were that man.' But his master was not there; he was staying, it appeared, at the house in Murrayfield; and though the butler would have been glad enough to have taken his place and given all the news of the family, John, struck with a little chill, was eager to be gone. Only, the door was scarce closed again, before he regretted that he had not asked about 'that man.'

He was to pay no more visits till he had seen his father and made all well at home; Alan had been the only possible exception, and John had not time to go as far as Murrayfield. But here he was on Regent Terrace; there was nothing to prevent him going round the end of the hill, and looking from without on the Mackenzies' house. As he went, he reflected that Flora must now be a woman of near his own age, and it was within the bounds of possibility that she was married; but this dishonourable doubt he dammed down.

There was the house, sure enough; but the door was of another colour, and what was this—two door-plates? He drew nearer; the top one bore, with dignified simplicity, the words, 'Mr. Proudfoot'; the lower one was more explicit, and informed the passer-by that here was likewise the abode of 'Mr. J. A. Dunlop Proudfoot, Advocate.' The Proudfoots must be rich, for no advocate could look to have much business in so remote a quarter; and John hated them for their wealth and for their name, and for the sake of the house they desecrated with their presence. He remembered a Proudfoot he had seen at school, not known: a little, whey-faced urchin, the despicable member of some lower class. Could it be this abortion that had climbed to be an advocate, and now lived in the birthplace

21

of Flora and the home of John's tenderest memories? The chill that had first seized upon him when he heard of Houston's absence deepened and struck inward. For a moment, as he stood under the doors of that estranged house, and looked east and west along the solitary pavement of the Royal Terrace, where not a cat was stirring, the sense of solitude and desolation took him by the throat, and he wished himself in San Francisco.

And then the figure he made, with his decent portliness, his whiskers, the money in his purse, the excellent cigar that he now lighted, recurred to his mind in consolatory comparison with that of a certain maddened lad who, on a certain spring Sunday ten years before, and in the hour of church-time silence, had stolen from that city by the Glasgow road. In the face of these changes, it were impious to doubt fortune's kindness. All would be well yet; the Mackenzies would be found, Flora, younger and lovelier and kinder than before; Alan would be found, and would have so nicely discriminated his behaviour as to have grown, on the one hand, into a valued friend of Mr. Nicholson's, and to have remained, upon the other, of that exact shade of joviality which John desired in his companions. And so, once more, John fell to work discounting the delightful future: his first appearance in the family pew; his first visit to his uncle Greig, who thought himself so great a financier, and on whose purblind Edinburgh eyes John was to let in the dazzling daylight of the West; and the details in general of that unrivalled transformation scene, in which he was to display to all Edinburgh a portly and successful gentleman in the shoes of the derided fugitive.

The time began to draw near when his father would have returned from the office, and it would be the prodigal's cue to enter. He strolled westward by Albany Street, facing the sunset embers, pleased, he knew not why, to move in that cold air and indigo twilight, starred with street-lamps. But there was one more disenchantment waiting him by the way.

At the corner of Pitt Street he paused to light a fresh cigar; the vesta threw, as he did so, a strong light upon his features, and a man of about his own age stopped at sight of it.

'I think your name must be Nicholson,' said the stranger.

It was too late to avoid recognition; and besides, as John was now actually on the way home, it hardly mattered, and he gave way to the impulse of his nature.

'Great Scott!' he cried, 'Beatson!' and shook hands with warmth. It scarce seemed he was repaid in kind.

'So you're home again?' said Beatson. 'Where have you been all this long time?'

'In the States,' said John—'California. I've made my pile though; and it suddenly struck me it would be a noble scheme to come home for Christmas.'

'I see,' said Beatson. 'Well, I hope we'll see something of you now you're here.'

'Oh, I guess so,' said John, a little frozen.

'Well, ta-ta,' concluded Beatson, and he shook hands again and went.

This was a cruel first experience. It was idle to blink facts: here was John home again, and Beatson—Old Beatson—did not care a rush. He recalled Old Beatson in the past—that merry and affectionate lad—and their joint adventures and mishaps, the window they had broken with a catapult in India Place, the escalade of the castle rock, and many another inestimable bond of friendship; and his hurt surprise grew deeper. Well, after all, it was only on a man's own family that he could count; blood was thicker than water, he remembered; and the net result of this encounter was to bring him to the doorstep of his father's house, with tenderer and softer feelings.

The night had come; the fanlight over the door shone bright; the two windows of the dining-room where the cloth was being laid, and the three windows of the drawing-room where Maria would be waiting dinner, glowed softlier through yellow blinds. It was like a vision of the past. All this time of his absence life had gone forward with an equal foot, and the fires and the gas had been lighted, and the meals spread, at the accustomed hours. At the accustomed hour, too, the bell had sounded thrice to call the family to worship. And at the thought, a pang of regret for his demerit seized him; he remembered the things that were good and that he had neglected, and the things that were evil and that he had loved; and it was with a prayer upon his lips that he mounted the steps and thrust the key into the key-hole.

He stepped into the lighted hall, shut the door softly behind him, and stood there fixed in wonder. No surprise of strangeness could

23

equal the surprise of that complete familiarity. There was the bust of Chalmers near the stair-railings, there was the clothes-brush in the accustomed place; and there, on the hat-stand, hung hats and coats that must surely be the same as he remembered. Ten years dropped from his life, as a pin may slip between the fingers; and the ocean and the mountains, and the mines, and crowded marts and mingled races of San Francisco, and his own fortune and his own disgrace, became, for that one moment, the figures of a dream that was over.

He took off his hat, and moved mechanically toward the stand; and there he found a small change that was a great one to him. The pin that had been his from boyhood, where he had flung his balmoral when he loitered home from the Academy, and his first hat when he came briskly back from college or the office—his pin was occupied. 'They might have at least respected my pin!' he thought, and he was moved as by a slight, and began at once to recollect that he was here an interloper, in a strange house, which he had entered almost by a burglary, and where at any moment he might be scandalously challenged.

He moved at once, his hat still in his hand, to the door of his father's room, opened it, and entered. Mr. Nicholson sat in the same place and posture as on that last Sunday morning; only he was older, and greyer, and sterner; and as he now glanced up and caught the eye of his son, a strange commotion and a dark flush sprang into his face.

'Father,' said John, steadily, and even cheerfully, for this was a moment against which he was long ago prepared, 'father, here I am, and here is the money that I took from you. I have come back to ask your forgiveness, and to stay Christmas with you and the children.'

'Keep your money,' said the father, 'and go!'

'Father!' cried John; 'for God's sake don't receive me this way. I've come for—'

'Understand me,' interrupted Mr. Nicholson; 'you are no son of mine; and in the sight of God, I wash my hands of you. One last thing I will tell you; one warning I will give you; all is discovered, and you are being hunted for your crimes; if you are still at large it is thanks to me; but I have done all that I mean to do; and from this time forth I would not raise one finger—not one finger—to save you from the gallows! And now,' with a low voice of absolute authority, and a single weighty gesture of the finger, 'and now—go!'

24

CHAPTER VI

THE HOUSE AT MURRAYFIELD

How John passed the evening, in what windy confusion of mind, in what squalls of anger and lulls of sick collapse, in what pacing of streets and plunging into public-houses, it would profit little to relate. His misery, if it were not progressive, yet tended in no way to diminish; for in proportion as grief and indignation abated, fear began to take their place. At first, his father's menacing words lay by in some safe drawer of memory, biding their hour. At first, John was all thwarted affection and blighted hope; next bludgeoned vanity raised its head again, with twenty mortal gashes: and the father was disowned even as he had disowned the son. What was this regular course of life, that John should have admired it? what were these clock-work virtues, from which love was absent? Kindness was the test, kindness the aim and soul; and judged by such a standard, the discarded prodigal—now rapidly drowning his sorrows and his reason in successive drams—was a creature of a lovelier morality than his self-righteous father. Yes, he was the better man; he felt it, glowed with the consciousness, and entering a public-house at the corner of Howard Place (whither he had somehow wandered) he pledged his own virtues in a glass—perhaps the fourth since his dismissal. Of that he knew nothing, keeping no account of what he did or where he went; and in the general crashing hurry of his nerves, unconscious of the approach of intoxication. Indeed, it is a question whether he were really growing intoxicated, or whether at first the spirits did not even sober him. For it was even as he drained this last glass that his father's ambiguous and menacing words—popping from their hiding-place in memory—startled him like a hand laid upon his shoulder. 'Crimes, hunted, the gallows.' They were ugly words; in the ears of an innocent man, perhaps all the uglier; for if some judicial error were in act against him, who should set a limit to its grossness or to how far it might be pushed? Not John, indeed; he was no believer in the powers of innocence, his cursed experience pointing in quite other ways; and his fears, once wakened, grew with every hour and hunted him about the city streets.

It was, perhaps, nearly nine at night; he had eaten nothing since

25

lunch, he had drunk a good deal, and he was exhausted by emotion, when the thought of Houston came into his head. He turned, not merely to the man as a friend, but to his house as a place of refuge. The danger that threatened him was still so vague that he knew neither what to fear nor where he might expect it; but this much at least seemed undeniable, that a private house was safer than a public inn. Moved by these counsels, he turned at once to the Caledonian Station, passed (not without alarm) into the bright lights of the approach, redeemed his portmanteau from the cloak-room, and was soon whirling in a cab along the Glasgow Road. The change of movement and position, the sight of the lamps twinkling to the rear, and the smell of damp and mould and rotten straw which clung about the vehicle, wrought in him strange alternations of lucidity and mortal giddiness.

'I have been drinking,' he discovered; 'I must go straight to bed, and sleep.' And he thanked Heaven for the drowsiness that came upon his mind in waves.

From one of these spells he was wakened by the stoppage of the cab; and, getting down, found himself in quite a country road, the last lamp of the suburb shining some way below, and the high walls of a garden rising before him in the dark. The Lodge (as the place was named), stood, indeed, very solitary. To the south it adjoined another house, but standing in so large a garden as to be well out of cry; on all other sides, open fields stretched upward to the woods of Corstorphine Hill, or backward to the dells of Ravelston, or downward toward the valley of the Leith. The effect of seclusion was aided by the great height of the garden walls, which were, indeed, conventual, and, as John had tested in former days, defied the climbing schoolboy. The lamp of the cab threw a gleam upon the door and the not brilliant handle of the bell.

'Shall I ring for ye?' said the cabman, who had descended from his perch, and was slapping his chest, for the night was bitter.

'I wish you would,' said John, putting his hand to his brow in one of his accesses of giddiness.

The man pulled at the handle, and the clanking of the bell replied from further in the garden; twice and thrice he did it, with sufficient intervals; in the great frosty silence of the night the sounds fell sharp and small.

'Does he expect ye?' asked the driver, with that manner of familiar interest that well became his port-wine face; and when John had told him no, 'Well, then,' said the cabman, 'if ye'll tak' my advice of it, we'll just gang back. And that's disinterested, mind ye, for my stables are in the Glesgie Road.'

'The servants must hear,' said John.

'Hout!' said the driver. 'He keeps no servants here, man. They're a' in the town house; I drive him often; it's just a kind of a hermitage, this.'

'Give me the bell,' said John; and he plucked at it like a man desperate.

The clamour had not yet subsided before they heard steps upon the gravel, and a voice of singular nervous irritability cried to them through the door, 'Who are you, and what do you want?'

'Alan,' said John, 'it's me—it's Fatty—John, you know. I'm just come home, and I've come to stay with you.'

There was no reply for a moment, and then the door was opened.

'Get the portmanteau down,' said John to the driver.

'Do nothing of the kind,' said Alan; and then to John, 'Come in here a moment. I want to speak to you.'

John entered the garden, and the door was closed behind him. A candle stood on the gravel walk, winking a little in the draughts; it threw inconstant sparkles on the clumped holly, struck the light and darkness to and fro like a veil on Alan's features, and sent his shadow hovering behind him. All beyond was inscrutable; and John's dizzy brain rocked with the shadow. Yet even so, it struck him that Alan was pale, and his voice, when he spoke, unnatural.

'What brings you here to-night?' he began. 'I don't want, God knows, to seem unfriendly; but I cannot take you in, Nicholson; I cannot do it.'

'Alan,' said John, 'you've just got to! You don't know the mess I'm in; the governor's turned me out, and I daren't show my face in an inn, because they're down on me for murder or something!'

'For what?' cried Alan, starting.

27

'Murder, I believe,' says John.

'Murder!' repeated Alan, and passed his hand over his eyes. 'What was that you were saying?' he asked again.

'That they were down on me,' said John. 'I'm accused of murder, by what I can make out; and I've really had a dreadful day of it, Alan, and I can't sleep on the roadside on a night like this—at least, not with a portmanteau,' he pleaded.

'Hush!' said Alan, with his head on one side; and then, 'Did you hear nothing?' he asked.

'No,' said John, thrilling, he knew not why, with communicated terror. 'No, I heard nothing; why?' And then, as there was no answer, he reverted to his pleading: 'But I say, Alan, you've just got to take me in. I'll go right away to bed if you have anything to do. I seem to have been drinking; I was that knocked over. I wouldn't turn you away, Alan, if you were down on your luck.'

'No?' returned Alan. 'Neither will you, then. Come and let's get your portmanteau.'

The cabman was paid, and drove off down the long, lamp-lighted hill, and the two friends stood on the side-walk beside the portmanteau till the last rumble of the wheels had died in silence. It seemed to John as though Alan attached importance to this departure of the cab; and John, who was in no state to criticise, shared profoundly in the feeling.

When the stillness was once more perfect, Alan shouldered the portmanteau, carried it in, and shut and locked the garden door; and then, once more, abstraction seemed to fall upon him, and he stood with his hand on the key, until the cold began to nibble at John's fingers.

'Why are we standing here?' asked John.

'Eh?' said Alan, blankly.

'Why, man, you don't seem yourself,' said the other.

'No, I'm not myself,' said Alan; and he sat down on the portmanteau and put his face in his hands.

John stood beside him swaying a little, and looking about him at the swaying shadows, the flitting sparkles, and the steady stars overhead, until the windless cold began to touch him through his clothes on the bare skin. Even in his bemused intelligence, wonder began to awake.

'I say, let's come on to the house,' he said at last.

'Yes, let's come on to the house,' repeated Alan.

And he rose at once, reshouldered the portmanteau, and taking the candle in his other hand, moved forward to the Lodge. This was a long, low building, smothered in creepers; and now, except for some chinks of light between the dining-room shutters, it was plunged in darkness and silence.

In the hall Alan lighted another candle, gave it to John, and opened the door of a bedroom.

'Here,' said he; 'go to bed. Don't mind me, John. You'll be sorry for me when you know.'

'Wait a bit,' returned John; 'I've got so cold with all that standing about. Let's go into the dining-room a minute. Just one glass to warm me, Alan.'

On the table in the hall stood a glass, and a bottle with a whisky label on a tray. It was plain the bottle had been just opened, for the cork and corkscrew lay beside it.

'Take that,' said Alan, passing John the whisky, and then with a certain roughness pushed his friend into the bedroom, and closed the door behind him.

John stood amazed; then he shook the bottle, and, to his further wonder, found it partly empty. Three or four glasses were gone. Alan must have uncorked a bottle of whisky and drank three or four glasses one after the other, without sitting down, for there was no chair, and that in his own cold lobby on this freezing night! It fully explained his eccentricities, John reflected sagely, as he mixed himself a grog. Poor Alan! He was drunk; and what a dreadful thing was drink, and what a slave to it poor Alan was, to drink in this unsociable, uncomfortable fashion! The man who would drink alone, except for health's sake—as John was now doing—was a man utterly lost. He took the grog out, and felt hazier, but warmer. It was hard work opening the portmanteau and finding his night

29

things; and before he was undressed, the cold had struck home to him once more. 'Well,' said he; 'just a drop more. There's no sense in getting ill with all this other trouble.' And presently dreamless slumber buried him.

When John awoke it was day. The low winter sun was already in the heavens, but his watch had stopped, and it was impossible to tell the hour exactly. Ten, he guessed it, and made haste to dress, dismal reflections crowding on his mind. But it was less from terror than from regret that he now suffered; and with his regret there were mingled cutting pangs of penitence. There had fallen upon him a blow, cruel, indeed, but yet only the punishment of old misdoing; and he had rebelled and plunged into fresh sin. The rod had been used to chasten, and he had bit the chastening fingers. His father was right; John had justified him; John was no guest for decent people's houses, and no fit associate for decent people's children. And had a broader hint been needed, there was the case of his old friend. John was no drunkard, though he could at times exceed; and the picture of Houston drinking neat spirits at his hall-table struck him with something like disgust. He hung back from meeting his old friend. He could have wished he had not come to him; and yet, even now, where else was he to turn?

These musings occupied him while he dressed, and accompanied him into the lobby of the house. The door stood open on the garden; doubtless, Alan had stepped forth; and John did as he supposed his friend had done. The ground was hard as iron, the frost still rigorous; as he brushed among the hollies, icicles jingled and glittered in their fall; and wherever he went, a volley of eager sparrows followed him. Here were Christmas weather and Christmas morning duly met, to the delight of children. This was the day of reunited families, the day to which he had so long looked forward, thinking to awake in his own bed in Randolph Crescent, reconciled with all men and repeating the footprints of his youth; and here he was alone, pacing the alleys of a wintry garden and filled with penitential thoughts.

And that reminded him: why was he alone? and where was Alan? The thought of the festal morning and the due salutations reawakened his desire for his friend, and he began to call for him by name. As the sound of his voice died away, he was aware of the greatness of the silence that environed him. But for the twittering of the sparrows and the crunching of his own feet upon the frozen snow, the whole windless world of air hung over him entranced, and the stillness weighed upon his mind with a horror of solitude.

30

Still calling at intervals, but now with a moderated voice, he made the hasty circuit of the garden, and finding neither man nor trace of man in all its evergreen coverts, turned at last to the house. About the house the silence seemed to deepen strangely. The door, indeed, stood open as before; but the windows were still shuttered, the chimneys breathed no stain into the bright air, there sounded abroad none of that low stir (perhaps audible rather to the ear of the spirit than to the ear of the flesh) by which a house announces and betrays its human lodgers. And yet Alan must be there—Alan locked in drunken slumbers, forgetful of the return of day, of the holy season, and of the friend whom he had so coldly received and was now so churlishly neglecting. John's disgust redoubled at the thought, but hunger was beginning to grow stronger than repulsion, and as a step to breakfast, if nothing else, he must find and arouse this sleeper.

He made the circuit of the bedroom quarters. All, until he came to Alan's chamber, were locked from without, and bore the marks of a prolonged disuse. But Alan's was a room in commission, filled with clothes, knickknacks, letters, books, and the conveniences of a solitary man. The fire had been lighted; but it had long ago burned out, and the ashes were stone cold. The bed had been made, but it had not been slept in.

Worse and worse, then; Alan must have fallen where he sat, and now sprawled brutishly, no doubt, upon the dining-room floor.

The dining-room was a very long apartment, and was reached through a passage; so that John, upon his entrance, brought but little light with him, and must move toward the windows with spread arms, groping and knocking on the furniture. Suddenly he tripped and fell his length over a prostrate body. It was what he had looked for, yet it shocked him; and he marvelled that so rough an impact should not have kicked a groan out of the drunkard. Men had killed themselves ere now in such excesses, a dreary and degraded end that made John shudder. What if Alan were dead? There would be a Christmas-day!

By this, John had his hand upon the shutters, and flinging them back, beheld once again the blessed face of the day. Even by that light the room had a discomfortable air. The chairs were scattered, and one had been overthrown; the table-cloth, laid as if for dinner, was twitched upon one side, and some of the dishes had fallen to the floor. Behind the table lay the drunkard, still unaroused, only one foot visible to John.

But now that light was in the room, the worst seemed over; it was a disgusting business, but not more than disgusting; and it was with no great apprehension that John proceeded to make the circuit of the table: his last comparatively tranquil moment for that day. No sooner had he turned the corner, no sooner had his eyes alighted on the body, than he gave a smothered, breathless cry, and fled out of the room and out of the house.

It was not Alan who lay there, but a man well up in years, of stern countenance and iron-grey locks; and it was no drunkard, for the body lay in a black pool of blood, and the open eyes stared upon the ceiling.

To and fro walked John before the door. The extreme sharpness of the air acted on his nerves like an astringent, and braced them swiftly. Presently, he not relaxing in his disordered walk, the images began to come clearer and stay longer in his fancy; and next the power of thought came back to him, and the horror and danger of his situation rooted him to the ground.

He grasped his forehead, and staring on one spot of gravel, pieced together what he knew and what he suspected. Alan had murdered some one: possibly 'that man' against whom the butler chained the door in Regent Terrace; possibly another; some one at least: a human soul, whom it was death to slay and whose blood lay spilled upon the floor. This was the reason of the whisky drinking in the passage, of his unwillingness to welcome John, of his strange behaviour and bewildered words; this was why he had started at and harped upon the name of murder; this was why he had stood and hearkened, or sat and covered his eyes, in the black night. And now he was gone, now he had basely fled; and to all his perplexities and dangers John stood heir.

'Let me think—let me think,' he said, aloud, impatiently, even pleadingly, as if to some merciless interrupter. In the turmoil of his wits, a thousand hints and hopes and threats and terrors dinning continuously in his ears, he was like one plunged in the hubbub of a crowd. How was he to remember—he, who had not a thought to spare—that he was himself the author, as well as the theatre, of so much confusion? But in hours of trial the junto of man's nature is dissolved, and anarchy succeeds.

It was plain he must stay no longer where he was, for here was a new Judicial Error in the very making. It was not so plain where he must go, for the old Judicial Error, vague as a cloud, appeared to fill

32

the habitable world; whatever it might be, it watched for him, full-grown, in Edinburgh; it must have had its birth in San Francisco; it stood guard, no doubt, like a dragon, at the bank where he should cash his credit; and though there were doubtless many other places, who should say in which of them it was not ambushed? No, he could not tell where he was to go; he must not lose time on these insolubilities. Let him go back to the beginning. It was plain he must stay no longer where he was. It was plain, too, that he must not flee as he was, for he could not carry his portmanteau, and to flee and leave it was to plunge deeper in the mire. He must go, leave the house unguarded, find a cab, and return—return after an absence? Had he courage for that?

And just then he spied a stain about a hand's-breadth on his trouser-leg, and reached his finger down to touch it. The finger was stained red: it was blood; he stared upon it with disgust, and awe, and terror, and in the sharpness of the new sensation, fell instantly to act.

He cleansed his finger in the snow, returned into the house, drew near with hushed footsteps to the dining-room door, and shut and locked it. Then he breathed a little freer, for here at least was an oaken barrier between himself and what he feared. Next, he hastened to his room, tore off the spotted trousers which seemed in his eyes a link to bind him to the gallows, flung them in a corner, donned another pair, breathlessly crammed his night things into his portmanteau, locked it, swung it with an effort from the ground, and with a rush of relief, came forth again under the open heavens.

The portmanteau, being of occidental build, was no feather-weight; it had distressed the powerful Alan; and as for John, he was crushed under its bulk, and the sweat broke upon him thickly. Twice he must set it down to rest before he reached the gate; and when he had come so far, he must do as Alan did, and take his seat upon one corner. Here then, he sat a while and panted; but now his thoughts were sensibly lightened; now, with the trunk standing just inside the door, some part of his dissociation from the house of crime had been effected, and the cabman need not pass the garden wall. It was wonderful how that relieved him; for the house, in his eyes, was a place to strike the most cursory beholder with suspicion, as though the very windows had cried murder.

But there was to be no remission of the strokes of fate. As he thus sat, taking breath in the shadow of the wall and hopped about by sparrows, it chanced that his eye roved to the fastening of the door;

33

and what he saw plucked him to his feet. The thing locked with a spring; once the door was closed, the bolt shut of itself; and without a key, there was no means of entering from without.

He saw himself obliged to one of two distasteful and perilous alternatives; either to shut the door altogether and set his portmanteau out upon the wayside, a wonder to all beholders; or to leave the door ajar, so that any thievish tramp or holiday schoolboy might stray in and stumble on the grisly secret. To the last, as the least desperate, his mind inclined; but he must first insure himself that he was unobserved. He peered out, and down the long road; it lay dead empty. He went to the corner of the by-road that comes by way of Dean; there also not a passenger was stirring. Plainly it was, now or never, the high tide of his affairs; and he drew the door as close as he durst, slipped a pebble in the chink, and made off downhill to find a cab.

Half-way down a gate opened, and a troop of Christmas children sallied forth in the most cheerful humour, followed more soberly by a smiling mother.

'And this is Christmas-day!' thought John; and could have laughed aloud in tragic bitterness of heart.

CHAPTER VII

A TRAGI-COMEDY IN A CAB

In front of Donaldson's Hospital, John counted it good fortune to perceive a cab a great way of, and by much shouting and waving of his arm, to catch the notice of the driver. He counted it good fortune, for the time was long to him till he should have done for ever with the Lodge; and the further he must go to find a cab, the greater the chance that the inevitable discovery had taken place, and that he should return to find the garden full of angry neighbours. Yet when the vehicle drew up he was sensibly chagrined to recognise the port-wine cabman of the night before. 'Here,' he could not but reflect, 'here is another link in the Judicial Error.'

The driver, on the other hand, was pleased to drop again upon so liberal a fare; and as he was a man—the reader must already have perceived—of easy, not to say familiar, manners, he dropped at once into a vein of friendly talk, commenting on the weather, on the sacred season, which struck him chiefly in the light of a day of liberal gratuities, on the chance which had reunited him to a pleasing customer, and on the fact that John had been (as he was pleased to call it) visibly 'on the randan' the night before.

'And ye look dreidful bad the-day, sir, I must say that,' he continued. 'There's nothing like a dram for ye—if ye'll take my advice of it; and bein' as it's Christmas, I'm no' saying,' he added, with a fatherly smile, 'but what I would join ye mysel'.'

John had listened with a sick heart.

'I'll give you a dram when we've got through,' said he, affecting a sprightliness which sat on him most unhandsomely, 'and not a drop till then. Business first, and pleasure afterward.'

With this promise the jarvey was prevailed upon to clamber to his place and drive, with hideous deliberation, to the door of the Lodge. There were no signs as yet of any public emotion; only, two men stood not far off in talk, and their presence, seen from afar, set John's pulses buzzing. He might have spared himself his fright, for the pair were lost in some dispute of a theological complexion, and

35

with lengthened upper lip and enumerating fingers, pursued the matter of their difference, and paid no heed to John.

But the cabman proved a thorn in the flesh.

Nothing would keep him on his perch; he must clamber down, comment upon the pebble in the door (which he regarded as an ingenious but unsafe device), help John with the portmanteau, and enliven matters with a flow of speech, and especially of questions, which I thus condense:—

'He'll no' be here himsel', will he? No? Well, he's an eccentric man—a fair oddity—if ye ken the expression. Great trouble with his tenants, they tell me. I've driven the fam'ly for years. I drove a cab at his father's waddin'. What'll your name be?—I should ken your face. Baigrey, ye say? There were Baigreys about Gilmerton; ye'll be one of that lot? Then this'll be a friend's portmantie, like? Why? Because the name upon it's Nucholson! Oh, if ye're in a hurry, that's another job. Waverley Brig? Are ye for away?'

So the friendly toper prated and questioned and kept John's heart in a flutter. But to this also, as to other evils under the sun, there came a period; and the victim of circumstances began at last to rumble toward the railway terminus at Waverley Bridge. During the transit, he sat with raised glasses in the frosty chill and mouldy fetor of his chariot, and glanced out sidelong on the holiday face of things, the shuttered shops, and the crowds along the pavement, much as the rider in the Tyburn cart may have observed the concourse gathering to his execution.

At the station his spirits rose again; another stage of his escape was fortunately ended—he began to spy blue water. He called a railway porter, and bade him carry the portmanteau to the cloak-room: not that he had any notion of delay; flight, instant flight was his design, no matter whither; but he had determined to dismiss the cabman ere he named, or even chose, his destination, thus possibly balking the Judicial Error of another link. This was his cunning aim, and now with one foot on the roadway, and one still on the coach-step, he made haste to put the thing in practice, and plunged his hand into his trousers pocket.

There was nothing there!

Oh yes; this time he was to blame. He should have remembered, and when he deserted his blood-stained pantaloons, he should not

36

have deserted along with them his purse. Make the most of his error, and then compare it with the punishment! Conceive his new position, for I lack words to picture it; conceive him condemned to return to that house, from the very thought of which his soul revolted, and once more to expose himself to capture on the very scene of the misdeed: conceive him linked to the mouldy cab and the familiar cabman. John cursed the cabman silently, and then it occurred to him that he must stop the incarceration of his portmanteau; that, at least, he must keep close at hand, and he turned to recall the porter. But his reflections, brief as they had appeared, must have occupied him longer than he supposed, and there was the man already returning with the receipt.

Well, that was settled; he had lost his portmanteau also; for the sixpence with which he had paid the Murrayfield Toll was one that had strayed alone into his waistcoat pocket, and unless he once more successfully achieved the adventure of the house of crime, his portmanteau lay in the cloakroom in eternal pawn, for lack of a penny fee. And then he remembered the porter, who stood suggestively attentive, words of gratitude hanging on his lips.

John hunted right and left; he found a coin—prayed God that it was a sovereign—drew it out, beheld a halfpenny, and offered it to the porter.

The man's jaw dropped.

'It's only a halfpenny!' he said, startled out of railway decency.

'I know that,' said John, piteously.

And here the porter recovered the dignity of man.

'Thank you, sir,' said he, and would have returned the base gratuity. But John, too, would none of it; and as they struggled, who must join in but the cabman?

'Hoots, Mr. Baigrey,' said he, 'you surely forget what day it is!'

'I tell you I have no change!' cried John.

'Well,' said the driver, 'and what then? I would rather give a man a shillin' on a day like this than put him off with a derision like a bawbee. I'm surprised at the like of you, Mr. Baigrey!'

'My name is not Baigrey!' broke out John, in mere childish temper and distress.

'Ye told me it was yoursel',' said the cabman.

'I know I did; and what the devil right had you to ask?' cried the unhappy one.

'Oh, very well,' said the driver. 'I know my place, if you know yours—if you know yours!' he repeated, as one who should imply grave doubt; and muttered inarticulate thunders, in which the grand old name of gentleman was taken seemingly in vain.

Oh to have been able to discharge this monster, whom John now perceived, with tardy clear-sightedness, to have begun betimes the festivities of Christmas! But far from any such ray of consolation visiting the lost, he stood bare of help and helpers, his portmanteau sequestered in one place, his money deserted in another and guarded by a corpse; himself, so sedulous of privacy, the cynosure of all men's eyes about the station; and, as if these were not enough mischances, he was now fallen in ill-blood with the beast to whom his poverty had linked him! In ill-blood, as he reflected dismally, with the witness who perhaps might hang or save him! There was no time to be lost; he durst not linger any longer in that public spot; and whether he had recourse to dignity or conciliation, the remedy must be applied at once. Some happily surviving element of manhood moved him to the former.

'Let us have no more of this,' said he, his foot once more upon the step. 'Go back to where we came from.'

He had avoided the name of any destination, for there was now quite a little band of railway folk about the cab, and he still kept an eye upon the court of justice, and laboured to avoid concentric evidence. But here again the fatal jarvey out-manoeuvred him.

'Back to the Ludge?' cried he, in shrill tones of protest.

'Drive on at once!' roared John, and slammed the door behind him, so that the crazy chariot rocked and jingled.

Forth trundled the cab into the Christmas streets, the fare within plunged in the blackness of a despair that neighboured on unconsciousness, the driver on the box digesting his rebuke and his customer's duplicity. I would not be thought to put the pair in competition; John's case was out of all parallel. But the cabman, too, is worth the sympathy of the judicious; for he was a fellow of genuine kindliness and a high sense of personal dignity incensed by drink; and his advances had been cruelly and publicly rebuffed. As he drove, therefore, he counted his wrongs, and thirsted for sympathy and drink. Now, it chanced he had a friend, a publican in Queensferry Street, from whom, in view of the sacredness of the occasion, he thought he might extract a dram. Queensferry Street lies something off the direct road to Murrayfield. But then there is the hilly cross-road that passes by the valley of the Leith and the Dean Cemetery; and Queensferry Street is on the way to that. What was to hinder the cabman, since his horse was dumb, from choosing the cross-road, and calling on his friend in passing? So it was decided; and the charioteer, already somewhat mollified, turned aside his horse to the right.

John, meanwhile, sat collapsed, his chin sunk upon his chest, his mind in abeyance. The smell of the cab was still faintly present to his senses, and a certain leaden chill about his feet, all else had disappeared in one vast oppression of calamity and physical faintness. It was drawing on to noon—two-and-twenty hours since he had broken bread; in the interval, he had suffered tortures of sorrow and alarm, and been partly tipsy; and though it was impossible to say he slept, yet when the cab stopped and the cabman thrust his head into the window, his attention had to be recalled from depths of vacancy.

'If you'll no' stand me a dram,' said the driver, with a well-merited severity of tone and manner, 'I dare say ye'll have no objection to my taking one mysel'?'

'Yes—no—do what you like,' returned John; and then, as he watched his tormentor mount the stairs and enter the whisky-shop, there floated into his mind a sense as of something long ago familiar. At that he started fully awake, and stared at the shop-fronts. Yes, he knew them; but when? and how? Long since, he thought; and then, casting his eye through the front glass, which had been recently occluded by the figure of the jarvey, he beheld the tree-tops of the rookery in Randolph Crescent. He was close to home—home, where he had thought, at that hour, to be sitting in the well-remembered drawing-room in friendly converse; and, instead—!

It was his first impulse to drop into the bottom of the cab; his next, to cover his face with his hands. So he sat, while the cabman toasted the publican, and the publican toasted the cabman, and both reviewed the affairs of the nation; so he still sat, when his master condescended to return, and drive off at last down-hill, along the curve of Lynedoch Place; but even so sitting, as he passed the end of his father's street, he took one glance from between shielding fingers, and beheld a doctor's carriage at the door.

'Well, just so,' thought he; 'I'll have killed my father! And this is Christmas-day!'

If Mr. Nicholson died, it was down this same road he must journey to the grave; and down this road, on the same errand, his wife had preceded him years before; and many other leading citizens, with the proper trappings and attendance of the end. And now, in that frosty, ill-smelling, straw-carpeted, and ragged-cushioned cab, with his breath congealing on the glasses, where else was John himself advancing to?

The thought stirred his imagination, which began to manufacture many thousand pictures, bright and fleeting, like the shapes in a kaleidoscope; and now he saw himself, ruddy and comfortered, sliding in the gutter; and, again, a little woe-begone, bored urchin tricked forth in crape and weepers, descending this same hill at the foot's pace of mourning coaches, his mother's body just preceding him; and yet again, his fancy, running far in front, showed him his destination—now standing solitary in the low sunshine, with the sparrows hopping on the threshold and the dead man within staring at the roof—and now, with a sudden change, thronged about with white-faced, hand-uplifting neighbours, and doctor bursting through their midst and fixing his stethoscope as he went, the policeman shaking a sagacious head beside the body. It was to this he feared that he was driving; in the midst of this he saw himself arrive, heard himself stammer faint explanations, and felt the hand of the constable upon his shoulder. Heavens! how he wished he had played the manlier part; how he despised himself that he had fled that fatal neighbourhood when all was quiet, and should now be tamely travelling back when it was thronging with avengers!

Any strong degree of passion lends, even to the dullest, the forces of the imagination. And so now as he dwelt on what was probably awaiting him at the end of this distressful drive—John, who saw things little, remembered them less, and could not have described them at all, beheld in his mind's-eye the garden of the Lodge, detailed as in a map; he went to and fro in it, feeding his terrors; he saw the hollies, the snowy borders, the paths where he had sought Alan, the high, conventual walls, the shut door—what! was the door shut? Ay, truly, he had shut it—shut in his money, his escape, his future life—shut it with these hands, and none could now open it! He heard the snap of the spring-lock like something bursting in his brain, and sat astonied.

And then he woke again, terror jarring through his vitals. This was no time to be idle; he must be up and doing, he must think. Once at the end of this ridiculous cruise, once at the Lodge door, there would be nothing for it but to turn the cab and trundle back again. Why, then, go so far? why add another feature of suspicion to a case already so suggestive? why not turn at once? It was easy to say, turn; but whither? He had nowhere now to go to; he could never— he saw it in letters of blood—he could never pay that cab; he was saddled with that cab for ever. Oh that cab! his soul yearned and burned, and his bowels sounded to be rid of it. He forgot all other cares. He must first quit himself of this ill-smelling vehicle and of the human beast that guided it—first do that; do that, at least; do that at once.

And just then the cab suddenly stopped, and there was his persecutor rapping on the front glass. John let it down, and beheld the port-wine countenance inflamed with intellectual triumph.

'I ken wha ye are!' cried the husky voice. 'I mind ye now. Ye're a Nucholson. I drove ye to Hermiston to a Christmas party, and ye came back on the box, and I let ye drive.'

It is a fact. John knew the man; they had been even friends. His enemy, he now remembered, was a fellow of great good nature— endless good nature—with a boy; why not with a man? Why not appeal to his better side? He grasped at the new hope.

'Great Scott! and so you did,' he cried, as if in a transport of delight, his voice sounding false in his own ears. 'Well, if that's so, I've something to say to you. I'll just get out, I guess. Where are we, any way?'

The driver had fluttered his ticket in the eyes of the branch-toll keeper, and they were now brought to on the highest and most solitary part of the by-road. On the left, a row of fieldside trees beshaded it; on the right, it was bordered by naked fallows, undulating down-hill to the Queensferry Road; in front, Corstorphine Hill raised its snow-bedabbled, darkling woods

41

against the sky. John looked all about him, drinking the clear air like wine; then his eyes returned to the cabman's face as he sat, not ungleefully, awaiting John's communication, with the air of one looking to be tipped.

The features of that face were hard to read, drink had so swollen them, drink had so painted them, in tints that varied from brick-red to mulberry. The small grey eyes blinked, the lips moved, with greed; greed was the ruling passion; and though there was some good nature, some genuine kindliness, a true human touch, in the old toper, his greed was now so set afire by hope, that all other traits of character lay dormant. He sat there a monument of gluttonous desire.

John's heart slowly fell. He had opened his lips, but he stood there and uttered nought. He sounded the well of his courage, and it was dry. He groped in his treasury of words, and it was vacant. A devil of dumbness had him by the throat; the devil of terror babbled in his ears; and suddenly, without a word uttered, with no conscious purpose formed in his will, John whipped about, tumbled over the roadside wall, and began running for his life across the fallows.

He had not gone far, he was not past the midst of the first afield, when his whole brain thundered within him, 'Fool! You have your watch!' The shock stopped him, and he faced once more toward the cab. The driver was leaning over the wall, brandishing his whip, his face empurpled, roaring like a bull. And John saw (or thought) that he had lost the chance. No watch would pacify the man's resentment now; he would cry for vengeance also. John would be had under the eye of the police; his tale would be unfolded, his secret plumbed, his destiny would close on him at last, and for ever.

He uttered a deep sigh; and just as the cabman, taking heart of grace, was beginning at last to scale the wall, his defaulting customer fell again to running, and disappeared into the further fields.

42

CHAPTER VIII

SINGULAR INSTANCE OF THE UTILITY OF PASS-KEYS

Where he ran at first, John never very clearly knew; nor yet how long a time elapsed ere he found himself in the by-road near the lodge of Ravelston, propped against the wall, his lungs heaving like bellows, his legs leaden-heavy, his mind possessed by one sole desire—to lie down and be unseen.   He remembered the thick coverts round the quarry-hole pond, an untrodden corner of the world where he might surely find concealment till the night should fall.   Thither he passed down the lane; and when he came there, behold! he had forgotten the frost, and the pond was alive with young people skating, and the pond-side coverts were thick with lookers-on.   He looked on a while himself.   There was one tall, graceful maiden, skating hand in hand with a youth, on whom she bestowed her bright eyes perhaps too patently; and it was strange with what anger John beheld her.   He could have broken forth in curses; he could have stood there, like a mortified tramp, and shaken his fist and vented his gall upon her by the hour—or so he thought; and the next moment his heart bled for the girl.   'Poor creature, it's little she knows!' he sighed.   'Let her enjoy herself while she can!'   But was it possible, when Flora used to smile at him on the Braid ponds, she could have looked so fulsome to a sick-hearted bystander?

The thought of one quarry, in his frozen wits, suggested another; and he plodded off toward Craigleith.   A wind had sprung up out of the north-west; it was cruel keen, it dried him like a fire, and racked his finger-joints.   It brought clouds, too; pale, swift, hurrying clouds, that blotted heaven and shed gloom upon the earth.   He scrambled up among the hazelled rubbish heaps that surround the caldron of the quarry, and lay flat upon the stones.   The wind searched close along the earth, the stones were cutting and icy, the bare hazels wailed about him; and soon the air of the afternoon began to be vocal with those strange and dismal harpings that herald snow.   Pain and misery turned in John's limbs to a harrowing impatience and blind desire of change; now he would roll in his harsh lair, and when the flints abraded him, was almost pleased; now he would

43

crawl to the edge of the huge pit and look dizzily down. He saw the spiral of the descending roadway, the steep crags, the clinging bushes, the peppering of snow-wreaths, and far down in the bottom, the diminished crane. Here, no doubt, was a way to end it. But it somehow did not take his fancy.

And suddenly he was aware that he was hungry; ay, even through the tortures of the cold, even through the frosts of despair, a gross, desperate longing after food, no matter what, no matter how, began to wake and spur him. Suppose he pawned his watch? But no, on Christmas-day—this was Christmas-day!—the pawnshop would be closed. Suppose he went to the public-house close by at Blackhall, and offered the watch, which was worth ten pounds, in payment for a meal of bread and cheese? The incongruity was too remarkable; the good folks would either put him to the door, or only let him in to send for the police. He turned his pockets out one after another; some San Francisco tram-car checks, one cigar, no lights, the pass-key to his father's house, a pocket-handkerchief, with just a touch of scent: no, money could be raised on none of these. There was nothing for it but to starve; and after all, what mattered it? That also was a door of exit.

He crept close among the bushes, the wind playing round him like a lash; his clothes seemed thin as paper, his joints burned, his skin curdled on his bones. He had a vision of a high-lying cattle-drive in California, and the bed of a dried stream with one muddy pool, by which the vaqueros had encamped: splendid sun over all, the big bonfire blazing, the strips of cow browning and smoking on a skewer of wood; how warm it was, how savoury the steam of scorching meat! And then again he remembered his manifold calamities, and burrowed and wallowed in the sense of his disgrace and shame. And next he was entering Frank's restaurant in Montgomery Street, San Francisco; he had ordered a pan-stew and venison chops, of which he was immoderately fond, and as he sat waiting, Munroe, the good attendant, brought him a whisky punch; he saw the strawberries float on the delectable cup, he heard the ice chink about the straws. And then he woke again to his detested fate, and found himself sitting, humped together, in a windy combe of quarry refuse—darkness thick about him, thin flakes of snow flying here and there like rags of paper, and the strong shuddering of his body clashing his teeth like a hiccough.

We have seen John in nothing but the stormiest condition; we have seen him reckless, desperate, tried beyond his moderate powers; of his daily self, cheerful, regular, not unthrifty, we have seen nothing; and it may thus be a surprise to the reader to learn that he was studiously careful of his health. This favourite preoccupation now awoke. If he were to sit there and die of cold, there would be mighty little gained; better the police cell and the chances of a jury trial, than the miserable certainty of death at a dyke-side before the next winter's dawn, or death a little later in the gas-lighted wards of an infirmary.

He rose on aching legs, and stumbled here and there among the rubbish heaps, still circumvented by the yawning crater of the quarry; or perhaps he only thought so, for the darkness was already dense, the snow was growing thicker, and he moved like a blind man, and with a blind man's terrors. At last he climbed a fence, thinking to drop into the road, and found himself staggering, instead, among the iron furrows of a ploughland, endless, it seemed, as a whole county. And next he was in a wood, beating among young trees; and then he was aware of a house with many lighted windows, Christmas carriages waiting at the doors, and Christmas drivers (for Christmas has a double edge) becoming swiftly hooded with snow. From this glimpse of human cheerfulness, he fled like Cain; wandered in the night, unpiloted, careless of whither he went; fell, and lay, and then rose again and wandered further; and at last, like a transformation scene, behold him in the lighted jaws of the city, staring at a lamp which had already donned the tilted night-cap of the snow. It came thickly now, a 'Feeding Storm'; and while he yet stood blinking at the lamp, his feet were buried. He remembered something like it in the past, a street-lamp crowned and caked upon the windward side with snow, the wind uttering its mournful hoot, himself looking on, even as now; but the cold had struck too sharply on his wits, and memory failed him as to the date and sequel of the reminiscence.

His next conscious moment was on the Dean Bridge; but whether he was John Nicholson of a bank in a California street, or some former John, a clerk in his father's office, he had now clean forgotten. Another blank, and he was thrusting his pass-key into the door-lock of his father's house.

Hours must have passed. Whether crouched on the cold stones or wandering in the fields among the snow, was more than he could tell; but hours had passed. The finger of the hall clock was close on twelve; a narrow peep of gas in the hall-lamp shed shadows; and the door of the back room—his father's room—was open and emitted a

45

warm light. At so late an hour, all this was strange; the lights should have been out, the doors locked, the good folk safe in bed. He marvelled at the irregularity, leaning on the hall-table; and marvelled to himself there; and thawed and grew once more hungry, in the warmer air of the house.

The clock uttered its premonitory catch; in five minutes Christmas-day would be among the days of the past—Christmas!—what a Christmas! Well, there was no use waiting; he had come into that house, he scarce knew how; if they were to thrust him forth again, it had best be done at once; and he moved to the door of the back room and entered.

Oh, well, then he was insane, as he had long believed.

There, in his father's room, at midnight, the fire was roaring and the gas blazing; the papers, the sacred papers—to lay a hand on which was criminal—had all been taken off and piled along the floor; a cloth was spread, and a supper laid, upon the business table; and in his father's chair a woman, habited like a nun, sat eating. As he appeared in the doorway, the nun rose, gave a low cry, and stood staring. She was a large woman, strong, calm, a little masculine, her features marked with courage and good sense; and as John blinked back at her, a faint resemblance dodged about his memory, as when a tune haunts us, and yet will not be recalled.

'Why, it's John!' cried the nun.

'I dare say I'm mad,' said John, unconsciously following King Lear; 'but, upon my word, I do believe you're Flora.'

'Of course I am,' replied she.

And yet it is not Flora at all, thought John; Flora was slender, and timid, and of changing colour, and dewy-eyed; and had Flora such an Edinburgh accent? But he said none of these things, which was perhaps as well. What he said was, 'Then why are you a nun?'

'Such nonsense!' said Flora. 'I'm a sick-nurse; and I am here nursing your sister, with whom, between you and me, there is precious little the matter. But that is not the question. The point is: How do you come here? and are you not ashamed to show yourself?'

'Flora,' said John, sepulchrally, 'I haven't eaten anything for three days. Or, at least, I don't know what day it is; but I guess I'm starving.'

46

'You unhappy man!' she cried. 'Here, sit down and eat my supper; and I'll just run upstairs and see my patient; not but what I doubt she's fast asleep, for Maria is a malade imaginaire.'

With this specimen of the French, not of Stratford-atte-Bowe, but of a finishing establishment in Moray Place, she left John alone in his father's sanctum. He fell at once upon the food; and it is to be supposed that Flora had found her patient wakeful, and been detained with some details of nursing, for he had time to make a full end of all there was to eat, and not only to empty the teapot, but to fill it again from a kettle that was fitfully singing on his father's fire. Then he sat torpid, and pleased, and bewildered; his misfortunes were then half forgotten; his mind considering, not without regret, this unsentimental return to his old love.

He was thus engaged, when that bustling woman noiselessly re-entered.

'Have you eaten?' said she. 'Then tell me all about it.'

It was a long and (as the reader knows) a pitiful story; but Flora heard it with compressed lips. She was lost in none of those questionings of human destiny that have, from time to time, arrested the flight of my own pen; for women, such as she, are no philosophers, and behold the concrete only. And women, such as she, are very hard on the imperfect man.

'Very well,' said she, when he had done; 'then down upon your knees at once, and beg God's forgiveness.'

And the great baby plumped upon his knees, and did as he was bid; and none the worse for that! But while he was heartily enough requesting forgiveness on general principles, the rational side of him distinguished, and wondered if, perhaps, the apology were not due upon the other part. And when he rose again from that becoming exercise, he first eyed the face of his old love doubtfully, and then, taking heart, uttered his protest.

'I must say, Flora,' said he, 'in all this business, I can see very little fault of mine.'

'If you had written home,' replied the lady, 'there would have been none of it. If you had even gone to Murrayfield reasonably sober, you would never have slept there, and the worst would not have happened. Besides, the whole thing began years ago. You got into

47

trouble, and when your father, honest man, was disappointed, you took the pet, or got afraid, and ran away from punishment. Well, you've had your own way of it, John, and I don't suppose you like it.'

'I sometimes fancy I'm not much better than a fool,' sighed John.

'My dear John,' said she, 'not much!'

He looked at her, and his eye fell. A certain anger rose within him; here was a Flora he disowned; she was hard; she was of a set colour; a settled, mature, undecorative manner; plain of speech, plain of habit—he had come near saying, plain of face. And this changeling called herself by the same name as the many-coloured, clinging maid of yore; she of the frequent laughter, and the many sighs, and the kind, stolen glances. And to make all worse, she took the upper hand with him, which (as John well knew) was not the true relation of the sexes. He steeled his heart against this sick-nurse.

'And how do you come to be here?' he asked.

She told him how she had nursed her father in his long illness, and when he died, and she was left alone, had taken to nurse others, partly from habit, partly to be of some service in the world; partly, it might be, for amusement. 'There's no accounting for taste,' said she. And she told him how she went largely to the houses of old friends, as the need arose; and how she was thus doubly welcome as an old friend first, and then as an experienced nurse, to whom doctors would confide the gravest cases.

'And, indeed, it's a mere farce my being here for poor Maria,' she continued; 'but your father takes her ailments to heart, and I cannot always be refusing him. We are great friends, your father and I; he was very kind to me long ago—ten years ago.

A strange stir came in John's heart. All this while had he been thinking only of himself? All this while, why had he not written to Flora? In penitential tenderness, he took her hand, and, to his awe and trouble, it remained in his, compliant. A voice told him this was Flora, after all—told him so quietly, yet with a thrill of singing.

'And you never married?' said he.

'No, John; I never married,' she replied.

The hall clock striking two recalled them to the sense of time.

48

'And now,' said she, 'you have been fed and warmed, and I have heard your story, and now it's high time to call your brother.'

'Oh!' cried John, chap-fallen; 'do you think that absolutely necessary?'

'I can't keep you here; I am a stranger,' said she. 'Do you want to run away again? I thought you had enough of that.'

He bowed his head under the reproof. She despised him, he reflected, as he sat once more alone; a monstrous thing for a woman to despise a man; and strangest of all, she seemed to like him. Would his brother despise him, too? And would his brother like him?

And presently the brother appeared, under Flora's escort; and, standing afar off beside the doorway, eyed the hero of this tale.

'So this is you?' he said, at length.

'Yes, Alick, it's me—it's John,' replied the elder brother, feebly.

'And how did you get in here?' inquired the younger.

'Oh, I had my pass-key,' says John.

'The deuce you had!' said Alexander. 'Ah, you lived in a better world! There are no pass-keys going now.'

'Well, father was always averse to them,' sighed John. And the conversation then broke down, and the brothers looked askance at one another in silence.

'Well, and what the devil are we to do?' said Alexander. 'I suppose if the authorities got wind of you, you would be taken up?'

'It depends on whether they've found the body or not,' returned John. 'And then there's that cabman, to be sure!'

'Oh, bother the body!' said Alexander. 'I mean about the other thing. That's serious.'

'Is that what my father spoke about?' asked John. 'I don't even know what it is.'

'About your robbing your bank in California, of course,' replied Alexander.

49

It was plain, from Flora's face, that this was the first she had heard of it; it was plainer still, from John's, that he was innocent.

'I!' he exclaimed. 'I rob my bank! My God! Flora, this is too much; even you must allow that.'

'Meaning you didn't?' asked Alexander.

'I never robbed a soul in all my days,' cried John: 'except my father, if you call that robbery; and I brought him back the money in this room, and he wouldn't even take it!'

'Look here, John,' said his brother, 'let us have no misunderstanding upon this. Macewen saw my father; he told him a bank you had worked for in San Francisco was wiring over the habitable globe to have you collared—that it was supposed you had nailed thousands; and it was dead certain you had nailed three hundred. So Macewen said, and I wish you would be careful how you answer. I may tell you also, that your father paid the three hundred on the spot.'

'Three hundred?' repeated John. 'Three hundred pounds, you mean? That's fifteen hundred dollars. Why, then, it's Kirkman!' he broke out. 'Thank Heaven! I can explain all that. I gave them to Kirkman to pay for me the night before I left—fifteen hundred dollars, and a letter to the manager. What do they suppose I would steal fifteen hundred dollars for? I'm rich; I struck it rich in stocks. It's the silliest stuff I ever heard of. All that's needful is to cable to the manager: Kirkman has the fifteen hundred—find Kirkman. He was a fellow-clerk of mine, and a hard case; but to do him justice, I didn't think he was as hard as this.'

'And what do you say to that, Alick?' asked Flora.

'I say the cablegram shall go to-night!' cried Alexander, with energy. 'Answer prepaid, too. If this can be cleared away—and upon my word I do believe it can—we shall all be able to hold up our heads again. Here, you John, you stick down the address of your bank manager. You, Flora, you can pack John into my bed, for which I have no further use to-night. As for me, I am off to the post-office, and thence to the High Street about the dead body. The police ought to know, you see, and they ought to know through John; and I can tell them some rigmarole about my brother being a man of highly nervous organisation, and the rest of it. And then, I'll tell you what, John—did you notice the name upon the cab?'

50

John gave the name of the driver, which, as I have not been able to command the vehicle, I here suppress.

'Well,' resumed Alexander, 'I'll call round at their place before I come back, and pay your shot for you. In that way, before breakfast-time, you'll be as good as new.'

John murmured inarticulate thanks. To see his brother thus energetic in his service moved him beyond expression; if he could not utter what he felt, he showed it legibly in his face; and Alexander read it there, and liked it the better in that dumb delivery.

'But there's one thing,' said the latter, 'cablegrams are dear; and I dare say you remember enough of the governor to guess the state of my finances.'

'The trouble is,' said John, 'that all my stamps are in that beastly house.'

'All your what?' asked Alexander.

'Stamps—money,' explained John. 'It's an American expression; I'm afraid I contracted one or two.'

'I have some,' said Flora. 'I have a pound note upstairs.'

'My dear Flora,' returned Alexander, 'a pound note won't see us very far; and besides, this is my father's business, and I shall be very much surprised if it isn't my father who pays for it.'

'I would not apply to him yet; I do not think that can be wise,' objected Flora.

'You have a very imperfect idea of my resources, and not at all of my effrontery,' replied Alexander. 'Please observe.'

He put John from his way, chose a stout knife among the supper things, and with surprising quickness broke into his father's drawer.

'There's nothing easier when you come to try,' he observed, pocketing the money.

'I wish you had not done that,' said Flora. 'You will never hear the last of it.'

'Oh, I don't know,' returned the young man; 'the governor is human after all. And now, John, let me see your famous pass-key. Get into bed, and don't move for any one till I come back. They won't mind you not answering when they knock; I generally don't myself.'

CHAPTER IX

IN WHICH MR. NICHOLSON ACCEPTS THE PRINCIPLE OF AN ALLOWANCE

In spite of the horrors of the day and the tea-drinking of the night, John slept the sleep of infancy. He was awakened by the maid, as it might have been ten years ago, tapping at the door. The winter sunrise was painting the east; and as the window was to the back of the house, it shone into the room with many strange colours of refracted light. Without, the houses were all cleanly roofed with snow; the garden walls were coped with it a foot in height; the greens lay glittering. Yet strange as snow had grown to John during his years upon the Bay of San Francisco, it was what he saw within that most affected him. For it was to his own room that Alexander had been promoted; there was the old paper with the device of flowers, in which a cunning fancy might yet detect the face of Skinny Jim, of the Academy, John's former dominie; there was the old chest of drawers; there were the chairs—one, two, three—three as before. Only the carpet was new, and the litter of Alexander's clothes and books and drawing materials, and a pencil-drawing on the wall, which (in John's eyes) appeared a marvel of proficiency.

He was thus lying, and looking, and dreaming, hanging, as it were, between two epochs of his life, when Alexander came to the door, and made his presence known in a loud whisper. John let him in, and jumped back into the warm bed.

'Well, John,' said Alexander, 'the cablegram is sent in your name, and twenty words of answer paid. I have been to the cab office and paid your cab, even saw the old gentleman himself, and properly apologised. He was mighty placable, and indicated his belief you had been drinking. Then I knocked up old Macewen out of bed, and explained affairs to him as he sat and shivered in a dressing-gown. And before that I had been to the High Street, where they have heard nothing of your dead body, so that I incline to the idea that you dreamed it.'

'Catch me!' said John.

'Well, the police never do know anything,' assented Alexander; 'and at any rate, they have despatched a man to inquire and to recover your trousers and your money, so that really your bill is now fairly clean; and I see but one lion in your path—the governor.'

'I'll be turned out again, you'll see,' said John, dismally.

'I don't imagine so,' returned the other; 'not if you do what Flora and I have arranged; and your business now is to dress, and lose no time about it. Is your watch right? Well, you have a quarter of an hour. By five minutes before the half-hour you must be at table, in your old seat, under Uncle Duthie's picture. Flora will be there to keep you countenance; and we shall see what we shall see.'

'Wouldn't it be wiser for me to stay in bed?' said John.

'If you mean to manage your own concerns, you can do precisely what you like,' replied Alexander; 'but if you are not in your place five minutes before the half-hour I wash my hands of you, for one.'

And thereupon he departed. He had spoken warmly, but the truth is, his heart was somewhat troubled. And as he hung over the balusters, watching for his father to appear, he had hard ado to keep himself braced for the encounter that must follow.

'If he takes it well, I shall be lucky,' he reflected.

'If he takes it ill, why it'll be a herring across John's tracks, and perhaps all for the best. He's a confounded muff, this brother of mine, but he seems a decent soul.'

At that stage a door opened below with a certain emphasis, and Mr. Nicholson was seen solemnly to descend the stairs, and pass into his own apartment. Alexander followed, quaking inwardly, but with a steady face. He knocked, was bidden to enter, and found his father standing in front of the forced drawer, to which he pointed as he spoke.

'This is a most extraordinary thing,' said he; 'I have been robbed!'

'I was afraid you would notice it,' observed his son; 'it made such a beastly hash of the table.'

'You were afraid I would notice it?' repeated Mr. Nicholson. 'And, pray, what may that mean?'

54

'That I was a thief, sir,' returned Alexander. 'I took all the money in case the servants should get hold of it; and here is the change, and a note of my expenditure. You were gone to bed, you see, and I did not feel at liberty to knock you up; but I think when you have heard the circumstances, you will do me justice. The fact is, I have reason to believe there has been some dreadful error about my brother John; the sooner it can be cleared up the better for all parties; it was a piece of business, sir—and so I took it, and decided, on my own responsibility, to send a telegram to San Francisco. Thanks to my quickness we may hear to-night. There appears to be no doubt, sir, that John has been abominably used.'

'When did this take place?' asked the father.

'Last night, sir, after you were asleep,' was the reply.

'It's most extraordinary,' said Mr. Nicholson. 'Do you mean to say you have been out all night?'

'All night, as you say, sir. I have been to the telegraph and the police office, and Mr. Macewen's. Oh, I had my hands full,' said Alexander.

'Very irregular,' said the father. 'You think of no one but yourself.'

'I do not see that I have much to gain in bringing back my elder brother,' returned Alexander, shrewdly.

The answer pleased the old man; he smiled. 'Well, well, I will go into this after breakfast,' said he.

'I'm sorry about the table,' said the son.

'The table is a small matter; I think nothing of that,' said the father.

'It's another example,' continued the son, 'of the awkwardness of a man having no money of his own. If I had a proper allowance, like other fellows of my age, this would have been quite unnecessary.'

'A proper allowance!' repeated his father, in tones of blighting sarcasm, for the expression was not new to him. 'I have never grudged you money for any proper purpose.'

'No doubt, no doubt,' said Alexander, 'but then you see you aren't always on the spot to have the thing explained to you. Last night, for instance—'

'You could have wakened me last night,' interrupted his father.

'Was it not some similar affair that first got John into a mess?' asked the son, skilfully evading the point.

But the father was not less adroit. 'And pray, sir, how did you come and go out of the house?' he asked.

'I forgot to lock the door, it seems,' replied Alexander.

'I have had cause to complain of that too often,' said Mr. Nicholson. 'But still I do not understand. Did you keep the servants up?'

'I propose to go into all that at length after breakfast,' returned Alexander. 'There is the half-hour going; we must not keep Miss Mackenzie waiting.'

And greatly daring, he opened the door.

Even Alexander, who, it must have been perceived was on terms of comparative freedom with his parent—even Alexander had never before dared to cut short an interview in this high-handed fashion. But the truth is, the very mass of his son's delinquencies daunted the old gentleman. He was like the man with the cart of apples— this was beyond him! That Alexander should have spoiled his table, taken his money, stayed out all night, and then coolly acknowledged all, was something undreamed of in the Nicholsonian philosophy, and transcended comment. The return of the change, which the old gentleman still carried in his hand, had been a feature of imposing impudence; it had dealt him a staggering blow. Then there was the reference to John's original flight—a subject which he always kept resolutely curtained in his own mind; for he was a man who loved to have made no mistakes, and when he feared he might have made one kept the papers sealed. In view of all these surprises and reminders, and of his son's composed and masterful demeanour, there began to creep on Mr. Nicholson a sickly misgiving. He seemed beyond his depth; if he did or said anything, he might come to regret it. The young man, besides, as he had pointed out himself, was playing a generous part. And if wrong had been done—and done to one who was, after, and in spite of, all, a Nicholson—it should certainly be righted.

All things considered, monstrous as it was to be cut short in his inquiries, the old gentleman submitted, pocketed the change, and followed his son into the dining-room. During these few steps he once more mentally revolted, and once more, and this time finally, laid down his arms: a still, small voice in his bosom having informed him authentically of a piece of news; that he was afraid of Alexander. The strange thing was that he was pleased to be afraid of him. He was proud of his son; he might be proud of him; the boy had character and grit, and knew what he was doing.

These were his reflections as he turned the corner of the dining-room door. Miss Mackenzie was in the place of honour, conjuring with a tea-pot and a cosy; and, behold! there was another person present, a large, portly, whiskered man of a very comfortable and respectable air, who now rose from his seat and came forward, holding out his hand.

'Good-morning, father,' said he.

Of the contention of feeling that ran high in Mr. Nicholson's starched bosom, no outward sign was visible; nor did he delay long to make a choice of conduct. Yet in that interval he had reviewed a great field of possibilities both past and future; whether it was possible he had not been perfectly wise in his treatment of John; whether it was possible that John was innocent; whether, if he turned John out a second time, as his outraged authority suggested, it was possible to avoid a scandal; and whether, if he went to that extremity, it was possible that Alexander might rebel.

'Hum!' said Mr. Nicholson, and put his hand, limp and dead, into John's.

And then, in an embarrassed silence, all took their places; and even the paper—from which it was the old gentleman's habit to suck mortification daily, as he marked the decline of our institutions—even the paper lay furled by his side.

But presently Flora came to the rescue. She slid into the silence with a technicality, asking if John still took his old inordinate amount of sugar. Thence it was but a step to the burning question of the day; and in tones a little shaken, she commented on the interval since she had last made tea for the prodigal, and congratulated him on his return. And then addressing Mr. Nicholson, she congratulated him also in a manner that defied his ill-humour; and from that launched into the tale of John's misadventures, not without some suitable suppressions.

Gradually Alexander joined; between them, whether he would or no,

57

they forced a word or two from John; and these fell so tremulously, and spoke so eloquently of a mind oppressed with dread, that Mr. Nicholson relented. At length even he contributed a question: and before the meal was at an end all four were talking even freely.

Prayers followed, with the servants gaping at this new-comer whom no one had admitted; and after prayers there came that moment on the clock which was the signal for Mr. Nicholson's departure.

'John,' said he, 'of course you will stay here. Be very careful not to excite Maria, if Miss Mackenzie thinks it desirable that you should see her. Alexander, I wish to speak with you alone.' And then, when they were both in the back room: 'You need not come to the office to-day,' said he; 'you can stay and amuse your brother, and I think it would be respectful to call on Uncle Greig. And by the bye' (this spoken with a certain—dare we say?—bashfulness), 'I agree to concede the principle of an allowance; and I will consult with Doctor Durie, who is quite a man of the world and has sons of his own, as to the amount. And, my fine fellow, you may consider yourself in luck!' he added, with a smile.

'Thank you,' said Alexander.

Before noon a detective had restored to John his money, and brought news, sad enough in truth, but perhaps the least sad possible. Alan had been found in his own house in Regent Terrace, under care of the terrified butler. He was quite mad, and instead of going to prison, had gone to Morningside Asylum. The murdered man, it appeared, was an evicted tenant who had for nearly a year pursued his late landlord with threats and insults; and beyond this, the cause and details of the tragedy were lost.

When Mr. Nicholson returned from dinner they were able to put a despatch into his hands: 'John V. Nicholson, Randolph Crescent, Edinburgh.—Kirkham has disappeared; police looking for him. All understood. Keep mind quite easy.—Austin.' Having had this explained to him, the old gentleman took down the cellar key and departed for two bottles of the 1820 port. Uncle Greig dined there that day, and Cousin Robina, and, by an odd chance, Mr. Macewen; and the presence of these strangers relieved what might have been otherwise a somewhat strained relation. Ere they departed, the family was welded once more into a fair semblance of unity.

In the end of April John led Flora—or, as more descriptive, Flora led John—to the altar, if altar that may be called which was indeed the drawing-room mantel-piece in Mr. Nicholson's house, with the Reverend Dr. Durie posted on the hearthrug in the guise of Hymen's priest.

The last I saw of them, on a recent visit to the north, was at a dinner-party in the house of my old friend Gellatly Macbride; and after we had, in classic phrase, 'rejoined the ladies,' I had an opportunity to overhear Flora conversing with another married woman on the much canvassed matter of a husband's tobacco.

'Oh yes!' said she; 'I only allow Mr. Nicholson four cigars a day. Three he smokes at fixed times—after a meal, you know, my dear; and the fourth he can take when he likes with any friend.'

'Bravo!' thought I to myself; 'this is the wife for my friend John!'

Every night in the year, four of us sat in the small parlour of the George at Debenham—the undertaker, and the landlord, and Fettes, and myself. Sometimes there would be more; but blow high, blow low, come rain or snow or frost, we four would be each planted in his own particular arm-chair. Fettes was an old drunken Scotchman, a man of education obviously, and a man of some property, since he lived in idleness. He had come to Debenham years ago, while still young, and by a mere continuance of living had grown to be an adopted townsman. His blue camlet cloak was a local antiquity, like the church-spire. His place in the parlour at the George, his absence from church, his old, crapulous, disreputable vices, were all things of course in Debenham. He had some vague Radical opinions and some fleeting infidelities, which he would now and again set forth and emphasise with tottering slaps upon the table. He drank rum—five glasses regularly every evening; and for the greater portion of his nightly visit to the George sat, with his glass in his right hand, in a state of melancholy alcoholic saturation. We called him the Doctor, for he was supposed to have some special knowledge of medicine, and had been known, upon a pinch, to set a fracture or reduce a dislocation; but beyond these slight particulars, we had no knowledge of his character and antecedents.

One dark winter night—it had struck nine some time before the landlord joined us—there was a sick man in the George, a great neighbouring proprietor suddenly struck down with apoplexy on his way to Parliament; and the great man's still greater London doctor had been telegraphed to his bedside. It was the first time that such a thing had happened in Debenham, for the railway was but newly open, and we were all proportionately moved by the occurrence.

'He's come,' said the landlord, after he had filled and lighted his pipe.

'He?' said I. 'Who?—not the doctor?'

'Himself,' replied our host.

'What is his name?'

'Doctor Macfarlane,' said the landlord.

Fettes was far through his third tumbler, stupidly fuddled, now nodding over, now staring mazily around him; but at the last word he seemed to awaken, and repeated the name 'Macfarlane' twice, quietly enough the first time, but with sudden emotion at the second.

'Yes,' said the landlord, 'that's his name, Doctor Wolfe Macfarlane.'

Fettes became instantly sober; his eyes awoke, his voice became clear, loud, and steady, his language forcible and earnest. We were all startled by the transformation, as if a man had risen from the dead.

'I beg your pardon,' he said, 'I am afraid I have not been paying much attention to your talk. Who is this Wolfe Macfarlane?' And then, when he had heard the landlord out, 'It cannot be, it cannot be,' he added; 'and yet I would like well to see him face to face.'

'Do you know him, Doctor?' asked the undertaker, with a gasp.

'God forbid!' was the reply. 'And yet the name is a strange one; it were too much to fancy two. Tell me, landlord, is he old?'

'Well,' said the host, 'he's not a young man, to be sure, and his hair is white; but he looks younger than you.'

'He is older, though; years older. But,' with a slap upon the table, 'it's the rum you see in my face—rum and sin. This man, perhaps, may have an easy conscience and a good digestion. Conscience! Hear me speak. You would think I was some good, old, decent Christian, would you not? But no, not I; I never canted. Voltaire might have canted if he'd stood in my shoes; but the brains'—with a rattling fillip on his bald head—'the brains were clear and active, and I saw and made no deductions.'

'If you know this doctor,' I ventured to remark, after a somewhat awful pause, 'I should gather that you do not share the landlord's good opinion.'

Fettes paid no regard to me.

'Yes,' he said, with sudden decision, 'I must see him face to face.'

There was another pause, and then a door was closed rather sharply on the first floor, and a step was heard upon the stair.

61

'That's the doctor,' cried the landlord. 'Look sharp, and you can catch him.'

It was but two steps from the small parlour to the door of the old George Inn; the wide oak staircase landed almost in the street; there was room for a Turkey rug and nothing more between the threshold and the last round of the descent; but this little space was every evening brilliantly lit up, not only by the light upon the stair and the great signal-lamp below the sign, but by the warm radiance of the bar-room window. The George thus brightly advertised itself to passers-by in the cold street. Fettes walked steadily to the spot, and we, who were hanging behind, beheld the two men meet, as one of them had phrased it, face to face. Dr. Macfarlane was alert and vigorous. His white hair set off his pale and placid, although energetic, countenance. He was richly dressed in the finest of broadcloth and the whitest of linen, with a great gold watch-chain, and studs and spectacles of the same precious material. He wore a broad-folded tie, white and speckled with lilac, and he carried on his arm a comfortable driving-coat of fur. There was no doubt but he became his years, breathing, as he did, of wealth and consideration; and it was a surprising contrast to see our parlour sot—bald, dirty, pimpled, and robed in his old camlet cloak—confront him at the bottom of the stairs.

'Macfarlane!' he said somewhat loudly, more like a herald than a friend.

The great doctor pulled up short on the fourth step, as though the familiarity of the address surprised and somewhat shocked his dignity.

'Toddy Macfarlane!' repeated Fettes.

The London man almost staggered. He stared for the swiftest of seconds at the man before him, glanced behind him with a sort of scare, and then in a startled whisper, 'Fettes!' he said, 'You!'

'Ay,' said the other, 'me! Did you think I was dead too? We are not so easy shut of our acquaintance.'

'Hush, hush!' exclaimed the doctor. 'Hush, hush! this meeting is so unexpected—I can see you are unmanned. I hardly knew you, I confess, at first; but I am overjoyed—overjoyed to have this opportunity. For the present it must be how-d'ye-do and good-bye in one, for my fly is waiting, and I must not fail the train; but you shall—let me see—yes—you shall give me your address, and you can count on early news of me. We must do something for you, Fettes. I fear you are out at elbows; but we must see to that for auld lang syne, as once we sang at suppers.'

'Money!' cried Fettes; 'money from you! The money that I had from you is lying where I cast it in the rain.'

Dr. Macfarlane had talked himself into some measure of superiority and confidence, but the uncommon energy of this refusal cast him back into his first confusion.

A horrible, ugly look came and went across his almost venerable countenance. 'My dear fellow,' he said, 'be it as you please; my last thought is to offend you. I would intrude on none. I will leave you my address, however—'

'I do not wish it—I do not wish to know the roof that shelters you,' interrupted the other. 'I heard your name; I feared it might be you; I wished to know if, after all, there were a God; I know now that there is none. Begone!'

He still stood in the middle of the rug, between the stair and doorway; and the great London physician, in order to escape, would be forced to step to one side. It was plain that he hesitated before the thought of this humiliation. White as he was, there was a dangerous glitter in his spectacles; but while he still paused uncertain, he became aware that the driver of his fly was peering in from the street at this unusual scene and caught a glimpse at the same time of our little body from the parlour, huddled by the corner of the bar. The presence of so many witnesses decided him at once to flee. He crouched together, brushing on the wainscot, and made a dart like a serpent, striking for the door. But his tribulation was not yet entirely at an end, for even as he was passing Fettes clutched him by the arm and these words came in a whisper, and yet painfully distinct, 'Have you seen it again?'

The great rich London doctor cried out aloud with a sharp, throttling cry; he dashed his questioner across the open space, and, with his hands over his head, fled out of the door like a detected thief. Before it had occurred to one of us to make a movement the fly was already rattling toward the station. The scene was over like a dream, but the dream had left proofs and traces of its passage. Next day the servant found the fine gold spectacles broken on the threshold, and that very night we were all standing breathless by the bar-room window, and Fettes at our side, sober, pale, and resolute in look.

'God protect us, Mr. Fettes!' said the landlord, coming first into possession of his customary senses. 'What in the universe is all this? These are strange things you have been saying.'

Fettes turned toward us; he looked us each in succession in the face. 'See if you can hold your tongues,' said he. 'That man Macfarlane is not safe to cross; those that have done so already have repented it too late.'

And then, without so much as finishing his third glass, far less waiting for the other two, he bade us good-bye and went forth, under the lamp of the hotel, into the black night.

We three turned to our places in the parlour, with the big red fire and four clear candles; and as we recapitulated what had passed, the first chill of our surprise soon changed into a glow of curiosity. We sat late; it was the latest session I have known in the old George. Each man, before we parted, had his theory that he was bound to prove; and none of us had any nearer business in this world than to track out the past of our condemned companion, and surprise the secret that he shared with the great London doctor. It is no great boast, but I believe I was a better hand at worming out a story than either of my fellows at the George; and perhaps there is now no other man alive who could narrate to you the following foul and unnatural events.

In his young days Fettes studied medicine in the schools of Edinburgh. He had talent of a kind, the talent that picks up swiftly what it hears and readily retails it for its own. He worked little at home; but he was civil, attentive, and intelligent in the presence of his masters. They soon picked him out as a lad who listened closely and remembered well; nay, strange as it seemed to me when I first heard it, he was in those days well favoured, and pleased by his exterior. There was, at that period, a certain extramural teacher of anatomy, whom I shall here designate by the letter K. His name was subsequently too well known. The man who bore it skulked through the streets of Edinburgh in disguise, while the mob that applauded at the execution of Burke called loudly for the blood of his employer. But Mr. K— was then at the top of his vogue; he enjoyed a popularity due partly to his own talent and address, partly to the incapacity of his rival, the university professor. The students, at least, swore by his name, and Fettes believed himself, and was

64

believed by others, to have laid the foundations of success when he had acquired the favour of this meteorically famous man. Mr. K— was a bon vivant as well as an accomplished teacher; he liked a sly illusion no less than a careful preparation. In both capacities Fettes enjoyed and deserved his notice, and by the second year of his attendance he held the half-regular position of second demonstrator or sub-assistant in his class.

In this capacity the charge of the theatre and lecture-room devolved in particular upon his shoulders. He had to answer for the cleanliness of the premises and the conduct of the other students, and it was a part of his duty to supply, receive, and divide the various subjects. It was with a view to this last—at that time very delicate—affair that he was lodged by Mr. K— in the same wynd, and at last in the same building, with the dissecting-rooms. Here, after a night of turbulent pleasures, his hand still tottering, his sight still misty and confused, he would be called out of bed in the black hours before the winter dawn by the unclean and desperate interlopers who supplied the table. He would open the door to these men, since infamous throughout the land. He would help them with their tragic burden, pay them their sordid price, and remain alone, when they were gone, with the unfriendly relics of humanity. From such a scene he would return to snatch another hour or two of slumber, to repair the abuses of the night, and refresh himself for the labours of the day.

Few lads could have been more insensible to the impressions of a life thus passed among the ensigns of mortality. His mind was closed against all general considerations. He was incapable of interest in the fate and fortunes of another, the slave of his own desires and low ambitions. Cold, light, and selfish in the last resort, he had that modicum of prudence, miscalled morality, which keeps a man from inconvenient drunkenness or punishable theft. He coveted, besides, a measure of consideration from his masters and his fellow-pupils, and he had no desire to fail conspicuously in the external parts of life. Thus he made it his pleasure to gain some distinction in his studies, and day after day rendered unimpeachable eye-service to his employer, Mr. K—. For his day of work he indemnified himself by nights of roaring, blackguardly enjoyment; and when that balance had been struck, the organ that he called his conscience declared itself content.

The supply of subjects was a continual trouble to him as well as to his master. In that large and busy class, the raw material of the anatomists kept perpetually running out; and the business thus rendered necessary was not only unpleasant in itself, but threatened dangerous consequences to all who were concerned. It was the policy of Mr. K— to ask no questions in his dealings with the trade. 'They bring the body, and we pay the price,' he used to say, dwelling on the alliteration—'quid pro quo.' And, again, and somewhat profanely, 'Ask no questions,' he would tell his assistants, 'for conscience' sake.' There was no understanding that the subjects were provided by the crime of murder. Had that idea been broached to him in words, he would have recoiled in horror; but the lightness of his speech upon so grave a matter was, in itself, an offence against good manners, and a temptation to the men with whom he dealt. Fettes, for instance, had often remarked to himself upon the singular freshness of the bodies. He had been struck again and again by the hang-dog, abominable looks of the ruffians who came to him before the dawn; and putting things together clearly in his private thoughts, he perhaps attributed a meaning too immoral and too categorical to the unguarded counsels of his master. He understood his duty, in short, to have three branches: to take what was brought, to pay the price, and to avert the eye from any evidence of crime.

One November morning this policy of silence was put sharply to the test. He had been awake all night with a racking toothache—pacing his room like a caged beast or throwing himself in fury on his bed— and had fallen at last into that profound, uneasy slumber that so often follows on a night of pain, when he was awakened by the third or fourth angry repetition of the concerted signal. There was a thin, bright moonshine; it was bitter cold, windy, and frosty; the town had not yet awakened, but an indefinable stir already preluded the noise and business of the day. The ghouls had come later than usual, and they seemed more than usually eager to be gone. Fettes, sick with sleep, lighted them upstairs. He heard their grumbling Irish voices through a dream; and as they stripped the sack from their sad merchandise he leaned dozing, with his shoulder propped against the wall; he had to shake himself to find the men their money. As he did so his eyes lighted on the dead face. He started; he took two steps nearer, with the candle raised.

'God Almighty!' he cried. 'That is Jane Galbraith!'

The men answered nothing, but they shuffled nearer the door.

'I know her, I tell you,' he continued. 'She was alive and hearty yesterday. It's impossible she can be dead; it's impossible you should have got this body fairly.'

'Sure, sir, you're mistaken entirely,' said one of the men.

But the other looked Fettes darkly in the eyes, and demanded the money on the spot.

It was impossible to misconceive the threat or to exaggerate the danger. The lad's heart failed him. He stammered some excuses, counted out the sum, and saw his hateful visitors depart. No sooner were they gone than he hastened to confirm his doubts. By a dozen unquestionable marks he identified the girl he had jested with the day before. He saw, with horror, marks upon her body that might well betoken violence. A panic seized him, and he took refuge in his room. There he reflected at length over the discovery that he had made; considered soberly the bearing of Mr. K—'s instructions and the danger to himself of interference in so serious a business, and at last, in sore perplexity, determined to wait for the advice of his immediate superior, the class assistant.

This was a young doctor, Wolfe Macfarlane, a high favourite among all the reckless students, clever, dissipated, and unscrupulous to the last degree. He had travelled and studied abroad. His manners were agreeable and a little forward. He was an authority on the stage, skilful on the ice or the links with skate or golf-club; he dressed with nice audacity, and, to put the finishing touch upon his glory, he kept a gig and a strong trotting-horse. With Fettes he was on terms of intimacy; indeed, their relative positions called for some community of life; and when subjects were scarce the pair would drive far into the country in Macfarlane's gig, visit and desecrate some lonely graveyard, and return before dawn with their booty to the door of the dissecting-room.

On that particular morning Macfarlane arrived somewhat earlier than his wont. Fettes heard him, and met him on the stairs, told him his story, and showed him the cause of his alarm. Macfarlane examined the marks on her body.

'Yes,' he said with a nod, 'it looks fishy.'

'Well, what should I do?' asked Fettes.

'Do?' repeated the other. 'Do you want to do anything? Least said soonest mended, I should say.'

'Some one else might recognise her,' objected Fettes. 'She was as well known as the Castle Rock.'

'We'll hope not,' said Macfarlane, 'and if anybody does—well, you didn't, don't you see, and there's an end. The fact is, this has been going on too long. Stir up the mud, and you'll get K— into the most unholy trouble; you'll be in a shocking box yourself. So will I, if you come to that. I should like to know how any one of us would look, or what the devil we should have to say for ourselves, in any Christian witness-box. For me, you know there's one thing certain—that, practically speaking, all our subjects have been murdered.'

'Macfarlane!' cried Fettes.

'Come now!' sneered the other. 'As if you hadn't suspected it yourself!'

'Suspecting is one thing—'

'And proof another. Yes, I know; and I'm as sorry as you are this should have come here,' tapping the body with his cane. 'The next best thing for me is not to recognise it; and,' he added coolly, 'I don't. You may, if you please. I don't dictate, but I think a man of the world would do as I do; and I may add, I fancy that is what K— would look for at our hands. The question is, Why did he choose us two for his assistants? And I answer, because he didn't want old wives.'

This was the tone of all others to affect the mind of a lad like Fettes. He agreed to imitate Macfarlane. The body of the unfortunate girl was duly dissected, and no one remarked or appeared to recognise her.

One afternoon, when his day's work was over, Fettes dropped into a popular tavern and found Macfarlane sitting with a stranger. This was a small man, very pale and dark, with coal-black eyes. The cut of his features gave a promise of intellect and refinement which was but feebly realised in his manners, for he proved, upon a nearer acquaintance, coarse, vulgar, and stupid. He exercised, however, a very remarkable control over Macfarlane; issued orders like the Great Bashaw; became inflamed at the least discussion or delay, and commented rudely on the servility with which he was obeyed. This most offensive person took a fancy to Fettes on the spot, plied him with drinks, and honoured him with unusual confidences on his past career. If a tenth part of what he confessed were true, he was a very loathsome rogue; and the lad's vanity was tickled by the attention of so experienced a man.

'I'm a pretty bad fellow myself,' the stranger remarked, 'but Macfarlane is the boy—Toddy Macfarlane I call him. Toddy, order your friend another glass.' Or it might be, 'Toddy, you jump up and shut the door.' 'Toddy hates me,' he said again. 'Oh yes, Toddy, you do!'

'Don't you call me that confounded name,' growled Macfarlane.

'Hear him! Did you ever see the lads play knife? He would like to do that all over my body,' remarked the stranger.

'We medicals have a better way than that,' said Fettes. 'When we dislike a dead friend of ours, we dissect him.'

Macfarlane looked up sharply, as though this jest were scarcely to his mind.

The afternoon passed. Gray, for that was the stranger's name, invited Fettes to join them at dinner, ordered a feast so sumptuous that the tavern was thrown into commotion, and when all was done commanded Macfarlane to settle the bill. It was late before they separated; the man Gray was incapably drunk. Macfarlane, sobered by his fury, chewed the cud of the money he had been forced to squander and the slights he had been obliged to swallow. Fettes, with various liquors singing in his head, returned home with devious footsteps and a mind entirely in abeyance. Next day Macfarlane was absent from the class, and Fettes smiled to himself as he imagined him still squiring the intolerable Gray from tavern to tavern. As soon as the hour of liberty had struck he posted from place to place in quest of his last night's companions. He could find them, however, nowhere; so returned early to his rooms, went early to bed, and slept the sleep of the just.

At four in the morning he was awakened by the well-known signal. Descending to the door, he was filled with astonishment to find Macfarlane with his gig, and in the gig one of those long and ghastly packages with which he was so well acquainted.

'What?' he cried. 'Have you been out alone? How did you manage?'

But Macfarlane silenced him roughly, bidding him turn to business. When they had got the body upstairs and laid it on the table,

Macfarlane made at first as if he were going away. Then he paused and seemed to hesitate; and then, 'You had better look at the face,' said he, in tones of some constraint. 'You had better,' he repeated, as Fettes only stared at him in wonder.

'But where, and how, and when did you come by it?' cried the other.

'Look at the face,' was the only answer.

Fettes was staggered; strange doubts assailed him. He looked from the young doctor to the body, and then back again. At last, with a start, he did as he was bidden. He had almost expected the sight that met his eyes, and yet the shock was cruel. To see, fixed in the rigidity of death and naked on that coarse layer of sackcloth, the man whom he had left well clad and full of meat and sin upon the threshold of a tavern, awoke, even in the thoughtless Fettes, some of the terrors of the conscience. It was a cras tibi which re-echoed in his soul, that two whom he had known should have come to lie upon these icy tables. Yet these were only secondary thoughts. His first concern regarded Wolfe. Unprepared for a challenge so momentous, he knew not how to look his comrade in the face. He durst not meet his eye, and he had neither words nor voice at his command.

It was Macfarlane himself who made the first advance. He came up quietly behind and laid his hand gently but firmly on the other's shoulder.

'Richardson,' said he, 'may have the head.'

Now Richardson was a student who had long been anxious for that portion of the human subject to dissect. There was no answer, and the murderer resumed: 'Talking of business, you must pay me; your accounts, you see, must tally.'

Fettes found a voice, the ghost of his own: 'Pay you!' he cried. 'Pay you for that?'

'Why, yes, of course you must. By all means and on every possible account, you must,' returned the other. 'I dare not give it for nothing, you dare not take it for nothing; it would compromise us both. This is another case like Jane Galbraith's. The more things are wrong the more we must act as if all were right. Where does old K— keep his money?'

'There,' answered Fettes hoarsely, pointing to a cupboard in the corner.

'Give me the key, then,' said the other, calmly, holding out his hand.

There was an instant's hesitation, and the die was cast. Macfarlane could not suppress a nervous twitch, the infinitesimal mark of an immense relief, as he felt the key between his fingers. He opened the cupboard, brought out pen and ink and a paper-book that stood in one compartment, and separated from the funds in a drawer a sum suitable to the occasion.

'Now, look here,' he said, 'there is the payment made—first proof of your good faith: first step to your security. You have now to clinch it by a second. Enter the payment in your book, and then you for your part may defy the devil.'

The next few seconds were for Fettes an agony of thought; but in balancing his terrors it was the most immediate that triumphed. Any future difficulty seemed almost welcome if he could avoid a present quarrel with Macfarlane. He set down the candle which he had been carrying all this time, and with a steady hand entered the date, the nature, and the amount of the transaction.

'And now,' said Macfarlane, 'it's only fair that you should pocket the lucre. I've had my share already. By the bye, when a man of the world falls into a bit of luck, has a few shillings extra in his pocket— I'm ashamed to speak of it, but there's a rule of conduct in the case. No treating, no purchase of expensive class-books, no squaring of old debts; borrow, don't lend.'

'Macfarlane,' began Fettes, still somewhat hoarsely, 'I have put my neck in a halter to oblige you.'

'To oblige me?' cried Wolfe. 'Oh, come! You did, as near as I can see the matter, what you downright had to do in self-defence. Suppose I got into trouble, where would you be? This second little matter flows clearly from the first. Mr. Gray is the continuation of Miss Galbraith. You can't begin and then stop. If you begin, you must keep on beginning; that's the truth. No rest for the wicked.'

A horrible sense of blackness and the treachery of fate seized hold upon the soul of the unhappy student.

'My God!' he cried, 'but what have I done? and when did I begin?

71

To be made a class assistant—in the name of reason, where's the harm in that? Service wanted the position; Service might have got it. Would he have been where I am now?'

'My dear fellow,' said Macfarlane, 'what a boy you are! What harm has come to you? What harm can come to you if you hold your tongue? Why, man, do you know what this life is? There are two squads of us—the lions and the lambs. If you're a lamb, you'll come to lie upon these tables like Gray or Jane Galbraith; if you're a lion, you'll live and drive a horse like me, like K—, like all the world with any wit or courage. You're staggered at the first. But look at K—! My dear fellow, you're clever, you have pluck. I like you, and K— likes you. You were born to lead the hunt; and I tell you, on my honour and my experience of life, three days from now you'll laugh at all these scarecrows like a High School boy at a farce.'

And with that Macfarlane took his departure and drove off up the wynd in his gig to get under cover before daylight. Fettes was thus left alone with his regrets. He saw the miserable peril in which he stood involved. He saw, with inexpressible dismay, that there was no limit to his weakness, and that, from concession to concession, he had fallen from the arbiter of Macfarlane's destiny to his paid and helpless accomplice. He would have given the world to have been a little braver at the time, but it did not occur to him that he might still be brave. The secret of Jane Galbraith and the cursed entry in the day-book closed his mouth.

Hours passed; the class began to arrive; the members of the unhappy Gray were dealt out to one and to another, and received without remark. Richardson was made happy with the head; and before the hour of freedom rang Fettes trembled with exultation to perceive how far they had already gone toward safety.

For two days he continued to watch, with increasing joy, the dreadful process of disguise.

On the third day Macfarlane made his appearance. He had been ill, he said; but he made up for lost time by the energy with which he directed the students. To Richardson in particular he extended the most valuable assistance and advice, and that student, encouraged by the praise of the demonstrator, burned high with ambitious hopes, and saw the medal already in his grasp.

Before the week was out Macfarlane's prophecy had been fulfilled. Fettes had outlived his terrors and had forgotten his baseness. He began to plume himself upon his courage, and had so arranged the story in his mind that he could look back on these events with an unhealthy pride. Of his accomplice he saw but little. They met, of course, in the business of the class; they received their orders together from Mr. K—. At times they had a word or two in private, and Macfarlane was from first to last particularly kind and jovial. But it was plain that he avoided any reference to their common secret; and even when Fettes whispered to him that he had cast in his lot with the lions and foresworn the lambs, he only signed to him smilingly to hold his peace.

At length an occasion arose which threw the pair once more into a closer union. Mr. K— was again short of subjects; pupils were eager, and it was a part of this teacher's pretensions to be always well supplied. At the same time there came the news of a burial in the rustic graveyard of Glencorse. Time has little changed the place in question. It stood then, as now, upon a cross road, out of call of human habitations, and buried fathom deep in the foliage of six cedar trees. The cries of the sheep upon the neighbouring hills, the streamlets upon either hand, one loudly singing among pebbles, the other dripping furtively from pond to pond, the stir of the wind in mountainous old flowering chestnuts, and once in seven days the voice of the bell and the old tunes of the precentor, were the only sounds that disturbed the silence around the rural church. The Resurrection Man—to use a byname of the period—was not to be deterred by any of the sanctities of customary piety. It was part of his trade to despise and desecrate the scrolls and trumpets of old tombs, the paths worn by the feet of worshippers and mourners, and the offerings and the inscriptions of bereaved affection. To rustic neighbourhoods, where love is more than commonly tenacious, and where some bonds of blood or fellowship unite the entire society of a parish, the body-snatcher, far from being repelled by natural respect, was attracted by the ease and safety of the task. To bodies that had been laid in earth, in joyful expectation of a far different awakening, there came that hasty, lamp-lit, terror-haunted resurrection of the spade and mattock. The coffin was forced, the cerements torn, and the melancholy relics, clad in sackcloth, after being rattled for hours on moonless byways, were at length exposed to uttermost indignities before a class of gaping boys.

Somewhat as two vultures may swoop upon a dying lamb, Fettes and Macfarlane were to be let loose upon a grave in that green and quiet resting-place. The wife of a farmer, a woman who had lived for sixty years, and been known for nothing but good butter and a godly conversation, was to be rooted from her grave at midnight and carried, dead and naked, to that far-away city that she had always honoured with her Sunday's best; the place beside her family was to be empty till the crack of doom; her innocent and almost venerable members to be exposed to that last curiosity of the anatomist.

Late one afternoon the pair set forth, well wrapped in cloaks and furnished with a formidable bottle. It rained without remission—a cold, dense, lashing rain. Now and again there blew a puff of wind, but these sheets of falling water kept it down. Bottle and all, it was a sad and silent drive as far as Penicuik, where they were to spend the evening. They stopped once, to hide their implements in a thick bush not far from the churchyard, and once again at the Fisher's Tryst, to have a toast before the kitchen fire and vary their nips of whisky with a glass of ale. When they reached their journey's end the gig was housed, the horse was fed and comforted, and the two young doctors in a private room sat down to the best dinner and the best wine the house afforded. The lights, the fire, the beating rain upon the window, the cold, incongruous work that lay before them, added zest to their enjoyment of the meal. With every glass their cordiality increased. Soon Macfarlane handed a little pile of gold to his companion.

'A compliment,' he said. 'Between friends these little d-d accommodations ought to fly like pipe-lights.'

Fettes pocketed the money, and applauded the sentiment to the echo. 'You are a philosopher,' he cried. 'I was an ass till I knew you. You and K— between you, by the Lord Harry! but you'll make a man of me.'

'Of course we shall,' applauded Macfarlane. 'A man? I tell you, it required a man to back me up the other morning. There are some big, brawling, forty-year-old cowards who would have turned sick at the look of the d-d thing; but not you—you kept your head. I watched you.'

'Well, and why not?' Fettes thus vaunted himself. 'It was no affair of mine. There was nothing to gain on the one side but disturbance, and on the other I could count on your gratitude, don't you see?' And he slapped his pocket till the gold pieces rang.

Macfarlane somehow felt a certain touch of alarm at these unpleasant words. He may have regretted that he had taught his young companion so successfully, but he had no time to interfere, for the other noisily continued in this boastful strain:—

'The great thing is not to be afraid. Now, between you and me, I don't want to hang—that's practical; but for all cant, Macfarlane, I was born with a contempt. Hell, God, Devil, right, wrong, sin, crime, and all the old gallery of curiosities—they may frighten boys, but men of the world, like you and me, despise them. Here's to the memory of Gray!'

It was by this time growing somewhat late. The gig, according to order, was brought round to the door with both lamps brightly shining, and the young men had to pay their bill and take the road. They announced that they were bound for Peebles, and drove in that direction till they were clear of the last houses of the town; then, extinguishing the lamps, returned upon their course, and followed a by-road toward Glencorse. There was no sound but that of their own passage, and the incessant, strident pouring of the rain. It was pitch dark; here and there a white gate or a white stone in the wall guided them for a short space across the night; but for the most part it was at a foot pace, and almost groping, that they picked their way through that resonant blackness to their solemn and isolated destination. In the sunken woods that traverse the neighbourhood of the burying-ground the last glimmer failed them, and it became necessary to kindle a match and re-illumine one of the lanterns of the gig. Thus, under the dripping trees, and environed by huge and moving shadows, they reached the scene of their unhallowed labours.

They were both experienced in such affairs, and powerful with the spade; and they had scarce been twenty minutes at their task before they were rewarded by a dull rattle on the coffin lid. At the same moment Macfarlane, having hurt his hand upon a stone, flung it carelessly above his head. The grave, in which they now stood almost to the shoulders, was close to the edge of the plateau of the graveyard; and the gig lamp had been propped, the better to illuminate their labours, against a tree, and on the immediate verge of the steep bank descending to the stream. Chance had taken a sure aim with the stone. Then came a clang of broken glass; night fell upon them; sounds alternately dull and ringing announced the bounding of the lantern down the bank, and its occasional collision with the trees. A stone or two, which it had dislodged in its descent, rattled behind it into the profundities of the glen; and then silence, like night, resumed its sway; and they might bend their hearing to its utmost pitch, but naught was to be heard except the rain, now marching to the wind, now steadily falling over miles of open country.

They were so nearly at an end of their abhorred task that they judged it wisest to complete it in the dark. The coffin was exhumed and broken open; the body inserted in the dripping sack and carried between them to the gig; one mounted to keep it in its place, and the other, taking the horse by the mouth, groped along by wall and bush until they reached the wider road by the Fisher's Tryst. Here was a faint, diffused radiancy, which they hailed like daylight; by that they pushed the horse to a good pace and began to rattle along merrily in the direction of the town.

They had both been wetted to the skin during their operations, and now, as the gig jumped among the deep ruts, the thing that stood propped between them fell now upon one and now upon the other. At every repetition of the horrid contact each instinctively repelled it with the greater haste; and the process, natural although it was, began to tell upon the nerves of the companions. Macfarlane made some ill-favoured jest about the farmer's wife, but it came hollowly from his lips, and was allowed to drop in silence. Still their unnatural burden bumped from side to side; and now the head would be laid, as if in confidence, upon their shoulders, and now the drenching sack-cloth would flap icily about their faces. A creeping chill began to possess the soul of Fettes. He peered at the bundle, and it seemed somehow larger than at first. All over the country-side, and from every degree of distance, the farm dogs accompanied their passage with tragic ululations; and it grew and grew upon his mind that some unnatural miracle had been accomplished, that some nameless change had befallen the dead body, and that it was in fear of their unholy burden that the dogs were howling.

'For God's sake,' said he, making a great effort to arrive at speech, 'for God's sake, let's have a light!'

Seemingly Macfarlane was affected in the same direction; for, though he made no reply, he stopped the horse, passed the reins to his companion, got down, and proceeded to kindle the remaining lamp. They had by that time got no farther than the cross-road down to Auchenclinny. The rain still poured as though the deluge were returning, and it was no easy matter to make a light in such a world of wet and darkness. When at last the flickering blue flame had been transferred to the wick and began to expand and clarify, and shed a wide circle of misty brightness round the gig, it became possible for the two young men to see each other and the thing they had along with them. The rain had moulded the rough sacking to the outlines of the body underneath; the head was distinct from the trunk, the shoulders plainly modelled; something at once spectral and human riveted their eyes upon the ghastly comrade of their drive.

For some time Macfarlane stood motionless, holding up the lamp. A nameless dread was swathed, like a wet sheet, about the body, and tightened the white skin upon the face of Fettes; a fear that was meaningless, a horror of what could not be, kept mounting to his brain. Another beat of the watch, and he had spoken. But his comrade forestalled him.

'That is not a woman,' said Macfarlane, in a hushed voice.

'It was a woman when we put her in,' whispered Fettes.

'Hold that lamp,' said the other. 'I must see her face.'

And as Fettes took the lamp his companion untied the fastenings of the sack and drew down the cover from the head. The light fell very clear upon the dark, well-moulded features and smooth-shaven cheeks of a too familiar countenance, often beheld in dreams of both of these young men. A wild yell rang up into the night; each leaped from his own side into the roadway: the lamp fell, broke, and was extinguished; and the horse, terrified by this unusual commotion, bounded and went off toward Edinburgh at a gallop, bearing along with it, sole occupant of the gig, the body of the dead and long-dissected Gray.

THE STORY OF A LIE

CHAPTER I

INTRODUCES THE ADMIRAL

When Dick Naseby was in Paris he made some odd acquaintances; for he was one of those who have ears to hear, and can use their eyes no less than their intelligence. He made as many thoughts as Stuart Mill; but his philosophy concerned flesh and blood, and was experimental as to its method. He was a type-hunter among mankind. He despised small game and insignificant personalities, whether in the shape of dukes or bagmen, letting them go by like sea-weed; but show him a refined or powerful face, let him hear a plangent or a penetrating voice, fish for him with a living look in some one's eye, a passionate gesture, a meaning and ambiguous smile, and his mind was instantaneously awakened. 'There was a man, there was a woman,' he seemed to say, and he stood up to the task of comprehension with the delight of an artist in his art.

And indeed, rightly considered, this interest of his was an artistic interest. There is no science in the personal study of human nature. All comprehension is creation; the woman I love is somewhat of my handiwork; and the great lover, like the great painter, is he that can so embellish his subject as to make her more than human, whilst yet by a cunning art he has so based his apotheosis on the nature of the case that the woman can go on being a true woman, and give her character free play, and show littleness, or cherish spite, or be greedy of common pleasures, and he continue to worship without a thought of incongruity. To love a character is only the heroic way of understanding it. When we love, by some noble method of our own or some nobility of mien or nature in the other, we apprehend the loved one by what is noblest in ourselves. When we are merely

78

studying an eccentricity, the method of our study is but a series of allowances. To begin to understand is to begin to sympathise; for comprehension comes only when we have stated another's faults and virtues in terms of our own. Hence the proverbial toleration of artists for their own evil creations. Hence, too, it came about that Dick Naseby, a high-minded creature, and as scrupulous and brave a gentleman as you would want to meet, held in a sort of affection the various human creeping things whom he had met and studied.

One of these was Mr. Peter Van Tromp, an English-speaking, two-legged animal of the international genus, and by profession of general and more than equivocal utility. Years before he had been a painter of some standing in a colony, and portraits signed 'Van Tromp' had celebrated the greatness of colonial governors and judges. In those days he had been married, and driven his wife and infant daughter in a pony trap. What were the steps of his declension? No one exactly knew. Here he was at least, and had been any time these past ten years, a sort of dismal parasite upon the foreigner in Paris.

It would be hazardous to specify his exact industry. Coarsely followed, it would have merited a name grown somewhat unfamiliar to our ears. Followed as he followed it, with a skilful reticence, in a kind of social chiaroscuro, it was still possible for the polite to call him a professional painter. His lair was in the Grand Hotel and the gaudiest cafés. There he might be seen jotting off a sketch with an air of some inspiration; and he was always affable, and one of the easiest of men to fall in talk withal. A conversation usually ripened into a peculiar sort of intimacy, and it was extraordinary how many little services Van Tromp contrived to render in the course of six-and-thirty hours. He occupied a position between a friend and a courier, which made him worse than embarrassing to repay. But those whom he obliged could always buy one of his villainous little pictures, or, where the favours had been prolonged and more than usually delicate, might order and pay for a large canvas, with perfect certainty that they would hear no more of the transaction.

Among resident artists he enjoyed celebrity of a non-professional sort. He had spent more money—no less than three individual fortunes, it was whispered—than any of his associates could ever hope to gain. Apart from his colonial career, he had been to Greece in a brigantine with four brass carronades; he had travelled Europe in a chaise and four, drawing bridle at the palace-doors of German princes; queens of song and dance had followed him like sheep and paid his tailor's bills. And to behold him now, seeking small loans with plaintive condescension, sponging for breakfast on an art-student of nineteen, a fallen Don Juan who had neglected to die at the propitious hour, had a colour of romance for young imaginations. His name and his bright past, seen through the prism of whispered gossip, had gained him the nickname of The Admiral.

Dick found him one day at the receipt of custom, rapidly painting a pair of hens and a cock in a little water-colour sketching box, and now and then glancing at the ceiling like a man who should seek inspiration from the muse. Dick thought it remarkable that a painter should choose to work over an absinthe in a public café, and looked the man over. The aged rakishness of his appearance was set off by a youthful costume; he had disreputable grey hair and a disreputable sore, red nose; but the coat and the gesture, the outworks of the man, were still designed for show. Dick came up to his table and inquired if he might look at what the gentleman was doing. No one was so delighted as the Admiral.

'A bit of a thing,' said he. 'I just dash them off like that. I—I dash them off,' he added with a gesture.

'Quite so,' said Dick, who was appalled by the feebleness of the production.

'Understand me,' continued Van Tromp; 'I am a man of the world. And yet—once an artist always an artist. All of a sudden a thought takes me in the street; I become its prey: it's like a pretty woman; no use to struggle; I must—dash it off.'

'I see,' said Dick.

'Yes,' pursued the painter; 'it all comes easily, easily to me; it is not my business; it's a pleasure. Life is my business—life—this great city, Paris—Paris after dark—its lights, its gardens, its odd corners. Aha!' he cried, 'to be young again! The heart is young, but the heels are leaden. A poor, mean business, to grow old! Nothing remains but the coup d'œil, the contemplative man's enjoyment, Mr. —,' and he paused for the name.

'Naseby,' returned Dick.

The other treated him at once to an exciting beverage, and expatiated on the pleasure of meeting a compatriot in a foreign land; to hear him, you would have thought they had encountered in

Central Africa. Dick had never found any one take a fancy to him so readily, nor show it in an easier or less offensive manner. He seemed tickled with him as an elderly fellow about town might be tickled by a pleasant and witty lad; he indicated that he was no precision, but in his wildest times had never been such a blade as he thought Dick. Dick protested, but in vain. This manner of carrying an intimacy at the bayonet's point was Van Tromp's stock-in-trade. With an older man he insinuated himself; with youth he imposed himself, and in the same breath imposed an ideal on his victim, who saw that he must work up to it or lose the esteem of this old and vicious patron. And what young man can bear to lose a character for vice?

At last, as it grew towards dinner-time, 'Do you know Paris?' asked Van Tromp.

'Not so well as you, I am convinced,' said Dick.

'And so am I,' returned Van Tromp gaily. 'Paris! My young friend— you will allow me?—when you know Paris as I do, you will have seen Strange Things. I say no more; all I say is, Strange Things. We are men of the world, you and I, and in Paris, in the heart of civilised existence. This is an opportunity, Mr. Naseby. Let us dine. Let me show you where to dine.'

Dick consented. On the way to dinner the Admiral showed him where to buy gloves, and made him buy them; where to buy cigars, and made him buy a vast store, some of which he obligingly accepted. At the restaurant he showed him what to order, with surprising consequences in the bill. What he made that night by his percentages it would be hard to estimate. And all the while Dick smilingly consented, understanding well that he was being done, but taking his losses in the pursuit of character as a hunter sacrifices his dogs. As for the Strange Things, the reader will be relieved to hear that they were no stranger than might have been expected, and he may find things quite as strange without the expense of a Van Tromp for guide. Yet he was a guide of no mean order, who made up for the poverty of what he had to show by a copious, imaginative commentary.

'And such,' said he, with a hiccup, 'such is Paris.'

'Pooh!' said Dick, who was tired of the performance.

The Admiral hung an ear, and looked up sidelong with a glimmer of suspicion.

81

'Good night,' said Dick; 'I'm tired.'

'So English!' cried Van Tromp, clutching him by the hand. 'So English! So blasé! Such a charming companion! Let me see you home.'

'Look here,' returned Dick, 'I have said good night, and now I'm going. You're an amusing old boy: I like you, in a sense; but here's an end of it for to-night. Not another cigar, not another grog, not another percentage out of me.'

'I beg your pardon!' cried the Admiral with dignity.

'Tut, man!' said Dick; 'you're not offended; you're a man of the world, I thought. I've been studying you, and it's over. Have I not paid for the lesson? Au revoir.'

Van Tromp laughed gaily, shook hands up to the elbows, hoped cordially they would meet again and that often, but looked after Dick as he departed with a tremor of indignation. After that they two not unfrequently fell in each other's way, and Dick would often treat the old boy to breakfast on a moderate scale and in a restaurant of his own selection. Often, too, he would lend Van Tromp the matter of a pound, in view of that gentleman's contemplated departure for Australia; there would be a scene of farewell almost touching in character, and a week or a month later they would meet on the same boulevard without surprise or embarrassment. And in the meantime Dick learned more about his acquaintance on all sides: heard of his yacht, his chaise and four, his brief season of celebrity amid a more confiding population, his daughter, of whom he loved to whimper in his cups, his sponging, parasitical, nameless way of life; and with each new detail something that was not merely interest nor yet altogether affection grew up in his mind towards this disreputable stepson of the arts. Ere he left Paris Van Tromp was one of those whom he entertained to a farewell supper; and the old gentleman made the speech of the evening, and then fell below the table, weeping, smiling, paralysed.

CHAPTER II

A LETTER TO THE PAPERS

Old Mr. Naseby had the sturdy, untutored nature of the upper middle class. The universe seemed plain to him. 'The thing's right,' he would say, or 'the thing's wrong'; and there was an end of it. There was a contained, prophetic energy in his utterances, even on the slightest affairs; he saw the damned thing; if you did not, it must be from perversity of will; and this sent the blood to his head. Apart from this, which made him an exacting companion, he was one of the most upright, hot-tempered, hot-headed old gentlemen in England. Florid, with white hair, the face of an old Jupiter, and the figure of an old fox-hunter, he enlivened the vale of Thyme from end to end on his big, cantering chestnut.

He had a hearty respect for Dick as a lad of parts. Dick had a respect for his father as the best of men, tempered by the politic revolt of a youth who has to see to his own independence. Whenever the pair argued, they came to an open rupture; and arguments were frequent, for they were both positive, and both loved the work of the intelligence. It was a treat to hear Mr. Naseby defending the Church of England in a volley of oaths, or supporting ascetic morals with an enthusiasm not entirely innocent of port wine. Dick used to wax indignant, and none the less so because, as his father was a skilful disputant, he found himself not seldom in the wrong. On these occasions, he would redouble in energy, and declare that black was white, and blue yellow, with much conviction and heat of manner; but in the morning such a licence of debate weighed upon him like a crime, and he would seek out his father, where he walked before breakfast on a terrace overlooking all the vale of Thyme.

'I have to apologise, sir, for last night—' he would begin.

'Of course you have,' the old gentleman would cut in cheerfully. 'You spoke like a fool. Say no more about it.'

'You do not understand me, sir. I refer to a particular point. I confess there is much force in your argument from the doctrine of possibilities.'

83

'Of course there is,' returned his father. 'Come down and look at the stables. Only,' he would add, 'bear this in mind, and do remember that a man of my age and experience knows more about what he is saying than a raw boy.'

He would utter the word 'boy' even more offensively than the average of fathers, and the light way in which he accepted these apologies cut Richard to the heart. The latter drew slighting comparisons, and remembered that he was the only one who ever apologised. This gave him a high station in his own esteem, and thus contributed indirectly to his better behaviour; for he was scrupulous as well as high-spirited, and prided himself on nothing more than on a just submission.

So things went on until the famous occasion when Mr. Naseby, becoming engrossed in securing the election of a sound party candidate to Parliament, wrote a flaming letter to the papers. The letter had about every demerit of party letters in general; it was expressed with the energy of a believer; it was personal; it was a little more than half unfair, and about a quarter untrue. The old man did not mean to say what was untrue, you may be sure; but he had rashly picked up gossip, as his prejudice suggested, and now rashly launched it on the public with the sanction of his name.

'The Liberal candidate,' he concluded, 'is thus a public turncoat. Is that the sort of man we want? He has been given the lie, and has swallowed the insult. Is that the sort of man we want? I answer No! With all the force of my conviction, I answer, No!'

And then he signed and dated the letter with an amateur's pride, and looked to be famous by the morrow.

Dick, who had heard nothing of the matter, was up first on that inauspicious day, and took the journal to an arbour in the garden. He found his father's manifesto in one column; and in another a leading article. 'No one that we are aware of,' ran the article, 'had consulted Mr. Naseby on the subject, but if he had been appealed to by the whole body of electors, his letter would be none the less ungenerous and unjust to Mr. Dalton. We do not choose to give the lie to Mr. Naseby, for we are too well aware of the consequences; but we shall venture instead to print the facts of both cases referred to by this red-hot partisan in another portion of our issue. Mr. Naseby is of course a large proprietor in our neighbourhood; but fidelity to facts, decent feeling, and English grammar, are all of them qualities more important than the possession of land. Mr. — is doubtless a great man; in his large gardens and that half-mile of greenhouses, where he has probably ripened his intellect and temper, he may say what he will to his hired vassals, but (as the Scotch say)—

here

He mauna think to domineer.

'Liberalism,' continued the anonymous journalist, 'is of too free and sound a growth,' etc.

Richard Naseby read the whole thing from beginning to end; and a crushing shame fell upon his spirit. His father had played the fool; he had gone out noisily to war, and come back with confusion. The moment that his trumpets sounded, he had been disgracefully unhorsed. There was no question as to the facts; they were one and all against the Squire. Richard would have given his ears to have suppressed the issue; but as that could not be done, he had his horse saddled, and furnishing himself with a convenient staff, rode off at once to Thymebury.

The editor was at breakfast in a large, sad apartment. The absence of furniture, the extreme meanness of the meal, and the haggard, bright-eyed, consumptive look of the culprit, unmanned our hero; but he clung to his stick, and was stout and warlike.

'You wrote the article in this morning's paper?' he demanded.

'You are young Mr. Naseby? I published it,' replied the editor, rising.

'My father is an old man,' said Richard; and then with an outburst, 'And a damned sight finer fellow than either you or Dalton!' He stopped and swallowed; he was determined that all should go with regularity. 'I have but one question to put to you, sir,' he resumed. 'Granted that my father was misinformed, would it not have been more decent to withhold the letter and communicate with him in private?'

'Believe me,' returned the editor, 'that alternative was not open to me. Mr. Naseby told me in a note that he had sent his letter to three other journals, and in fact threatened me with what he called exposure if I kept it back from mine. I am really concerned at what has happened; I sympathise and approve of your emotion, young gentleman; but the attack on Mr. Dalton was gross, very gross, and I had no choice but to offer him my columns to reply. Party has its duties, sir,' added the scribe, kindling, as one who should propose a sentiment; 'and the attack was gross.'

Richard stood for half a minute digesting the answer; and then the god of fair play came upper-most in his heart, and murmuring 'Good morning,' he made his escape into the street.

His horse was not hurried on the way home, and he was late for breakfast. The Squire was standing with his back to the fire in a state bordering on apoplexy, his fingers violently knitted under his coat tails. As Richard came in, he opened and shut his mouth like a cod-fish, and his eyes protruded.

'Have you seen that, sir?' he cried, nodding towards the paper.

'Yes, sir,' said Richard.

'Oh, you've read it, have you?'

'Yes, I have read it,' replied Richard, looking at his foot.

'Well,' demanded the old gentleman, 'and what have you to say to it, sir?'

'You seem to have been misinformed,' said Dick.

'Well? What then? Is your mind so sterile, sir? Have you not a word of comment? no proposal?'

'I fear, sir, you must apologise to Mr. Dalton. It would be more handsome, indeed it would be only just, and a free acknowledgment would go far—' Richard paused, no language appearing delicate enough to suit the case.

'That is a suggestion which should have come from me, sir,' roared the father. 'It is out of place upon your lips. It is not the thought of a loyal son. Why, sir, if my father had been plunged in such deplorable circumstances, I should have thrashed the editor of that vile sheet within an inch of his life. I should have thrashed the man, sir. It would have been the action of an ass; but it would have shown that I had the blood and the natural affections of a man. Son? You are no son, no son of mine, sir!'

'Sir!' said Dick.

86

'I'll tell you what you are, sir,' pursued the Squire. 'You're a Benthamite. I disown you. Your mother would have died for shame; there was no modern cant about your mother; she thought— she said to me, sir—I'm glad she's in her grave, Dick Naseby. Misinformed! Misinformed, sir? Have you no loyalty, no spring, no natural affections? Are you clockwork, hey? Away! This is no place for you. Away!' (waving his hands in the air). 'Go away! Leave me!'

At this moment Dick beat a retreat in a disarray of nerves, a whistling and clamour of his own arteries, and in short in such a final bodily disorder as made him alike incapable of speech or hearing. And in the midst of all this turmoil, a sense of unpardonable injustice remained graven in his memory.

CHAPTER III
IN THE ADMIRAL'S NAME

There was no return to the subject. Dick and his father were henceforth on terms of coldness. The upright old gentleman grew more upright when he met his son, buckrammed with immortal anger; he asked after Dick's health, and discussed the weather and the crops with an appalling courtesy; his pronunciation was point-de-vice, his voice was distant, distinct, and sometimes almost trembling with suppressed indignation.

As for Dick, it seemed to him as if his life had come abruptly to an end. He came out of his theories and clevernesses; his premature man-of-the-worldness, on which he had prided himself on his travels, 'shrank like a thing ashamed' before this real sorrow. Pride, wounded honour, pity and respect tussled together daily in his heart; and now he was within an ace of throwing himself upon his father's mercy, and now of slipping forth at night and coming back no more to Naseby House. He suffered from the sight of his father, nay, even from the neighbourhood of this familiar valley, where every corner had its legend, and he was besieged with memories of childhood. If he fled into a new land, and among none but strangers, he might escape his destiny, who knew? and begin again light-heartedly. From that chief peak of the hills, that now and then, like an uplifted finger, shone in an arrow of sunlight through the broken clouds, the shepherd in clear weather might perceive the shining of the sea. There, he thought, was hope. But his heart failed him when he saw the Squire; and he remained. His fate was not that of the voyager by sea and land; he was to travel in the spirit, and begin his journey sooner than he supposed.

For it chanced one day that his walk led him into a portion of the uplands which was almost unknown to him. Scrambling through some rough woods, he came out upon a moorland reaching towards the hills. A few lofty Scotch firs grew hard by upon a knoll; a clear fountain near the foot of the knoll sent up a miniature streamlet which meandered in the heather. A shower had just skimmed by, but now the sun shone brightly, and the air smelt of the pines and the grass. On a stone under the trees sat a young lady sketching.

88

We have learned to think of women in a sort of symbolic transfiguration, based on clothes; and one of the readiest ways in which we conceive our mistress is as a composite thing, principally petticoats. But humanity has triumphed over clothes; the look, the touch of a dress has become alive; and the woman who stitched herself into these material integuments has now permeated right through and gone out to the tip of her skirt. It was only a black dress that caught Dick Naseby's eye; but it took possession of his mind, and all other thoughts departed. He drew near, and the girl turned round. Her face startled him; it was a face he wanted; and he took it in at once like breathing air.

'I beg your pardon,' he said, taking off his hat, 'you are sketching.'

'Oh!' she exclaimed, 'for my own amusement. I despise the thing.'

'Ten to one, you do yourself injustice,' returned Dick. 'Besides, it's a freemasonry. I sketch myself, and you know what that implies.'

'No. What?' she asked.

'Two things,' he answered. 'First, that I am no very difficult critic; and second, that I have a right to see your picture.'

She covered the block with both her hands. 'Oh no,' she said; 'I am ashamed.'

'Indeed, I might give you a hint,' said Dick. 'Although no artist myself, I have known many; in Paris I had many for friends, and used to prowl among studios.'

'In Paris?' she cried, with a leap of light into her eyes. 'Did you ever meet Mr. Van Tromp?'

'I? Yes. Why, you're not the Admiral's daughter, are you?'

'The Admiral? Do they call him that?' she cried. 'Oh, how nice, how nice of them! It is the younger men who call him so, is it not?'

'Yes,' said Dick, somewhat heavily.

'You can understand now,' she said, with an unspeakable accent of contented noble-minded pride, 'why it is I do not choose to show my sketch. Van Tromp's daughter! The Admiral's daughter! I delight in that name. The Admiral! And so you know my father?'

89

'Well,' said Dick, 'I met him often; we were even intimate. He may have mentioned my name—Naseby.'

'He writes so little. He is so busy, so devoted to his art! I have had a half wish,' she added laughing, 'that my father was a plainer man, whom I could help—to whom I could be a credit; but only sometimes, you know, and with only half my heart. For a great painter! You have seen his works?'

'I have seen some of them,' returned Dick; 'they—they are very nice.'

She laughed aloud. 'Nice?' she repeated. 'I see you don't care much for art.'

'Not much,' he admitted; 'but I know that many people are glad to buy Mr. Van Tromp's pictures.'

'Call him the Admiral!' she cried. 'It sounds kindly and familiar; and I like to think that he is appreciated and looked up to by young painters. He has not always been appreciated; he had a cruel life for many years; and when I think'—there were tears in her eyes—'when I think of that, I feel incline to be a fool,' she broke off. 'And now I shall go home. You have filled me full of happiness; for think, Mr. Naseby, I have not seen my father since I was six years old; and yet he is in my thoughts all day! You must come and call on me; my aunt will be delighted, I am sure; and then you will tell me all—all about my father, will you not?'

Dick helped her to get her sketching traps together; and when all was ready, she gave Dick her hand and a frank return of pressure.

'You are my father's friend,' she said; 'we shall be great friends too. You must come and see me soon.'

Then she was gone down the hillside at a run; and Dick stood by himself in a state of some bewilderment and even distress. There were elements of laughter in the business; but the black dress, and the face that belonged to it, and the hand that he had held in his, inclined him to a serious view. What was he, under the circumstances, called upon to do? Perhaps to avoid the girl? Well, he would think about that. Perhaps to break the truth to her? Why, ten to one, such was her infatuation, he would fail. Perhaps to keep up the illusion, to colour the raw facts; to help her to false ideas, while yet not plainly stating falsehoods? Well, he would see about that; he would also see about avoiding the girl. He saw about this last so well, that the next afternoon beheld him on his way to visit her.

In the meantime the girl had gone straight home, light as a bird, tremulous with joy, to the little cottage where she lived alone with a maiden aunt; and to that lady, a grim, sixty years old Scotchwoman, with a nodding head, communicated news of her encounter and invitation.

'A friend of his?' cried the aunt. 'What like is he? What did ye say was his name?'

She was dead silent, and stared at the old woman darkling. Then very slowly, 'I said he was my father's friend; I have invited him to my house, and come he shall,' she said; and with that she walked off to her room, where she sat staring at the wall all the evening. Miss M'Glashan, for that was the aunt's name, read a large bible in the kitchen with some of the joys of martyrdom.

It was perhaps half-past three when Dick presented himself, rather scrupulously dressed, before the cottage door; he knocked, and a voice bade him enter. The kitchen, which opened directly off the garden, was somewhat darkened by foliage; but he could see her as she approached from the far end to meet him. This second sight of her surprised him. Her strong black brows spoke of temper easily aroused and hard to quiet; her mouth was small, nervous and weak; there was something dangerous and sulky underlying, in her nature, much that was honest, compassionate, and even noble.

'My father's name,' she said, 'has made you very welcome.'

And she gave him her hand, with a sort of curtsy. It was a pretty greeting, although somewhat mannered; and Dick felt himself among the gods. She led him through the kitchen to a parlour, and presented him to Miss M'Glashan.

'Esther,' said the aunt, 'see and make Mr. Naseby his tea.'

And as soon as the girl was gone upon this hospitable intent, the old woman crossed the room and came quite near to Dick as if in menace.

'Ye know that man?' she asked in an imperious whisper.

'Mr. Van Tromp?' said Dick. 'Yes, I know him.'

91

'Well, and what brings ye here?' she said. 'I couldn't save the mother—her that's dead—but the bairn!' She had a note in her voice that filled poor Dick with consternation. 'Man,' she went on, 'what is it now? Is it money?'

'My dear lady,' said Dick, 'I think you misinterpret my position. I am young Mr. Naseby of Naseby House. My acquaintance with Mr. Van Tromp is really very slender; I am only afraid that Miss Van Tromp has exaggerated our intimacy in her own imagination. I know positively nothing of his private affairs, and do not care to know. I met him casually in Paris—that is all.'

Miss M'Glashan drew along breath. 'In Paris?' she said. 'Well, and what do you think of him?—what do ye think of him?' she repeated, with a different scansion, as Richard, who had not much taste for such a question, kept her waiting for an answer.

'I found him a very agreeable companion,' he said.

'Ay,' said she, 'did ye! And how does he win his bread?'

'I fancy,' he gasped, 'that Mr. Van Tromp has many generous friends.'

'I'll warrant!' she sneered; and before Dick could find more to say, she was gone from the room.

Esther returned with the tea-things, and sat down.

'Now,' she said cosily, 'tell me all about my father.'

'He'—stammered Dick, 'he is a very agreeable companion.'

'I shall begin to think it is more than you are, Mr. Naseby,' she said, with a laugh. 'I am his daughter, you forget. Begin at the beginning, and tell me all you have seen of him, all he said and all you answered. You must have met somewhere; begin with that.'

So with that he began: how he had found the Admiral painting in a café; how his art so possessed him that he could not wait till he got home to—well, to dash off his idea; how (this in reply to a question) his idea consisted of a cock crowing and two hens eating corn; how he was fond of cocks and hens; how this did not lead him to neglect more ambitious forms of art; how he had a picture in his studio of a Greek subject which was said to be remarkable from several points of view; how no one had seen it nor knew the precise site of the studio in which it was being vigorously though secretly confected; how (in answer to a suggestion) this shyness was common to the Admiral, Michelangelo, and others; how they (Dick and Van Tromp) had struck up an acquaintance at once, and dined together that same night; how he (the Admiral) had once given money to a beggar; how he spoke with effusion of his little daughter; how he had once borrowed money to send her a doll—a trait worthy of Newton, she being then in her nineteenth year at least; how, if the doll never arrived (which it appeared it never did), the trait was only more characteristic of the highest order of creative intellect; how he was—no, not beautiful—striking, yes, Dick would go so far, decidedly striking in appearance; how his boots were made to lace and his coat was black, not cut-away, a frock; and so on, and so on by the yard. It was astonishing how few lies were necessary. After all, people exaggerated the difficulty of life. A little steering, just a touch of the rudder now and then, and with a willing listener there is no limit to the domain of equivocal speech. Sometimes Miss M'Glashan made a freezing sojourn in the parlour; and then the task seemed unaccountably more difficult; but to Esther, who was all eyes and ears, her face alight with interest, his stream of language flowed without break or stumble, and his mind was ever fertile in ingenious evasions and—

What an afternoon it was for Esther!

'Ah!' she said at last, 'it's good to hear all this! My aunt, you should know, is narrow and too religious; she cannot understand an artist's life. It does not frighten me,' she added grandly; 'I am an artist's daughter.'

With that speech, Dick consoled himself for his imposture; she was not deceived so grossly after all; and then if a fraud, was not the fraud piety itself?—and what could be more obligatory than to keep alive in the heart of a daughter that filial trust and honour which, even although misplaced, became her like a jewel of the mind? There might be another thought, a shade of cowardice, a selfish desire to please; poor Dick was merely human; and what would you have had him do?

93

CHAPTER IV

ESTHER ON THE FILIAL RELATION

A month later Dick and Esther met at the stile beside the cross roads; had there been any one to see them but the birds and summer insects, it would have been remarked that they met after a different fashion from the day before. Dick took her in his arms, and their lips were set together for a long while. Then he held her at arm's-length, and they looked straight into each other's eyes.

'Esther!' he said; you should have heard his voice!

'Dick!' said she.

'My darling!'

It was some time before they started for their walk; he kept an arm about her, and their sides were close together as they walked; the sun, the birds, the west wind running among the trees, a pressure, a look, the grasp tightening round a single finger, these things stood them in lieu of thought and filled their hearts with joy. The path they were following led them through a wood of pine-trees carpeted with heather and blue-berry, and upon this pleasant carpet, Dick, not without some seriousness, made her sit down.

'Esther!' he began, 'there is something you ought to know. You know my father is a rich man, and you would think, now that we love each other, we might marry when we pleased. But I fear, darling, we may have long to wait, and shall want all our courage.'

'I have courage for anything,' she said, 'I have all I want; with you and my father, I am so well off, and waiting is made so happy, that I could wait a lifetime and not weary.'

He had a sharp pang at the mention of the Admiral. 'Hear me out,' he continued. 'I ought to have told you this before; but it is a thought I shrink from; if it were possible, I should not tell you even now. My poor father and I are scarce on speaking terms.'

'Your father,' she repeated, turning pale.

94

'It must sound strange to you; but yet I cannot think I am to blame,' he said. 'I will tell you how it happened.'

'Oh Dick!' she said, when she had heard him to an end, 'how brave you are, and how proud. Yet I would not be proud with a father. I would tell him all.'

'What!' cried Dick, 'go in months after, and brag that I had meant to thrash the man, and then didn't. And why? Because my father had made a bigger ass of himself than I supposed. My dear, that's nonsense.'

She winced at his words and drew away. 'But when that is all he asks,' she pleaded. 'If he only knew that you had felt that impulse, it would make him so proud and happy. He would see you were his own son after all, and had the same thoughts and the same chivalry of spirit. And then you did yourself injustice when you spoke just now. It was because the editor was weak and poor and excused himself, that you repented your first determination. Had he been a big red man, with whiskers, you would have beaten him—you know you would—if Mr. Naseby had been ten times more committed. Do you think, if you can tell it to me, and I understand at once, that it would be more difficult to tell it to your own father, or that he would not be more ready to sympathise with you than I am? And I love you, Dick; but then he is your father.'

'My dear,' said Dick, desperately, 'you do not understand; you do not know what it is to be treated with daily want of comprehension and daily small injustices, through childhood and boyhood and manhood, until you despair of a hearing, until the thing rides you like a nightmare, until you almost hate the sight of the man you love, and who's your father after all. In short, Esther, you don't know what it is to have a father, and that's what blinds you.'

'I see,' she said musingly, 'you mean that I am fortunate in my father. But I am not so fortunate after all; you forget, I do not know him; it is you who know him; he is already more your father than mine.' And here she took his hand. Dick's heart had grown as cold as ice. 'But I am sorry for you, too,' she continued, 'it must be very sad and lonely.'

'You misunderstand me,' said Dick, chokingly. 'My father is the best man I know in all this world; he is worth a hundred of me, only he doesn't understand me, and he can't be made to.'

There was a silence for a while. 'Dick,' she began again, 'I am going to ask a favour, it's the first since you said you loved me. May I see your father—see him pass, I mean, where he will not observe me?'

'Why?' asked Dick.

'It is a fancy; you forget, I am romantic about fathers.'

The hint was enough for Dick; he consented with haste, and full of hang-dog penitence and disgust, took her down by a backway and planted her in the shrubbery, whence she might see the Squire ride by to dinner. There they both sat silent, but holding hands, for nearly half an hour. At last the trotting of a horse sounded in the distance, the park gates opened with a clang, and then Mr. Naseby appeared, with stooping shoulders and a heavy, bilious countenance, languidly rising to the trot. Esther recognised him at once; she had often seen him before, though with her huge indifference for all that lay outside the circle of her love, she had never so much as wondered who he was; but now she recognised him, and found him ten years older, leaden and springless, and stamped by an abiding sorrow.

'Oh Dick, Dick!' she said, and the tears began to shine upon her face as she hid it in his bosom; his own fell thickly too. They had a sad walk home, and that night, full of love and good counsel, Dick exerted every art to please his father, to convince him of his respect and affection, to heal up this breach of kindness, and reunite two hearts. But alas! the Squire was sick and peevish; he had been all day glooming over Dick's estrangement—for so he put it to himself, and now with growls, cold words, and the cold shoulder, he beat off all advances, and entrenched himself in a just resentment.

CHAPTER V

THE PRODIGAL FATHER MAKES HIS
DEBUT AT HOME

That took place upon a Tuesday. On the Thursday following, as Dick was walking by appointment, earlier than usual, in the direction of the cottage, he was appalled to meet in the lane a fly from Thymebury, containing the human form of Miss M'Glashan. The lady did not deign to remark him in her passage; her face was suffused with tears, and expressed much concern for the packages by which she was surrounded. He stood still, and asked himself what this circumstance might portend. It was so beautiful a day that he was loth to forecast evil, yet something must perforce have happened at the cottage, and that of a decisive nature; for here was Miss M'Glashan on her travels, with a small patrimony in brown paper parcels, and the old lady's bearing implied hot battle and unqualified defeat. Was the house to be closed against him? Was Esther left alone, or had some new protector made his appearance from among the millions of Europe? It is the character of love to loathe the near relatives of the loved one; chapters in the history of the human race have justified this feeling, and the conduct of uncles, in particular, has frequently met with censure from the independent novelist. Miss M'Glashan was now seen in the rosy colours of regret; whoever succeeded her, Dick felt the change would be for the worse. He hurried forward in this spirit; his anxiety grew upon him with every step; as he entered the garden a voice fell upon his ear, and he was once more arrested, not this time by doubt, but by indubitable certainty of ill.

The thunderbolt had fallen; the Admiral was here.

Dick would have retreated, in the panic terror of the moment; but Esther kept a bright look-out when her lover was expected. In a twinkling she was by his side, brimful of news and pleasure, too glad to notice his embarrassment, and in one of those golden transports of exultation which transcend not only words but caresses. She took him by the end of the fingers (reaching forward to take them, for her great preoccupation was to save time), she drew him towards her, pushed him past her in the door, and planted him face to face with

Mr. Van Tromp, in a suit of French country velveteens and with a remarkable carbuncle on his nose. Then, as though this was the end of what she could endure in the way of joy, Esther turned and ran out of the room.

The two men remained looking at each other with some confusion on both sides. Van Tromp was naturally the first to recover; he put out his hand with a fine gesture.

'And you know my little lass, my Esther?' he said. 'This is pleasant; this is what I have conceived of home. A strange word for the old rover; but we all have a taste for home and the home-like, disguise it how we may. It has brought me here, Mr. Naseby,' he concluded, with an intonation that would have made his fortune on the stage, so just, so sad, so dignified, so like a man of the world and a philosopher, 'and you see a man who is content.'

'I see,' said Dick.

'Sit down,' continued the parasite, setting the example. 'Fortune has gone against me. (I am just sirrupping a little brandy—after my journey.) I was going down, Mr. Naseby; between you and me, I was décavé; I borrowed fifty francs, smuggled my valise past the concierge—a work of considerable tact—and here I am!'

'Yes,' said Dick; 'and here you are.' He was quite idiotic.

Esther, at this moment, re-entered the room.

'Are you glad to see him?' she whispered in his ear, the pleasure in her voice almost bursting through the whisper into song.

'Oh yes,' said Dick, 'very.'

'I knew you would be,' she replied; 'I told him how you loved him.'

'Help yourself,' said the Admiral, 'help yourself; and let us drink to a new existence.'

'To a new existence,' repeated Dick; and he raised the tumbler to his lips, but set it down untasted. He had had enough of novelties for one day.

Esther was sitting on a stool beside her father's feet, holding her knees in her arms, and looking with pride from one to the other of her two visitors. Her eyes were so bright that you were never sure if there were tears in them or not; little voluptuous shivers ran about her body; sometimes she nestled her chin into her throat, sometimes threw back her head, with ecstasy; in a word, she was in that state when it is said of people that they cannot contain themselves for happiness. It would be hard to exaggerate the agony of Richard.

And, in the meantime, Van Tromp ran on interminably.

'I never forget a friend,' said he, 'nor yet an enemy: of the latter, I never had but two—myself and the public; and I fancy I have had my vengeance pretty freely out of both.' He chuckled. 'But those days are done. Van Tromp is no more. He was a man who had successes; I believe you knew I had successes—to which we shall refer no farther,' pulling down his neckcloth with a smile. 'That man exists no more: by an exercise of will I have destroyed him. There is something like it in the poets. First, a brilliant and conspicuous career—the observed, I may say, of all observers, including the bum-bailie: and then, presto! a quiet, sly, old, rustic bonhomme, cultivating roses. In Paris, Mr. Naseby—'

'Call him Richard, father,' said Esther.

'Richard, if he will allow me. Indeed, we are old friends, and now near neighbours; and, à propos, how are we off for neighbours, Richard? The cottage stands, I think, upon your father's land—a family which I respect—and the wood, I understand, is Lord Trevanion's. Not that I care; I am an old Bohemian. I have cut society with a cut direct; I cut it when I was prosperous, and now I reap my reward, and can cut it with dignity in my declension. These are our little amours propres, my daughter: your father must respect himself. Thank you, yes; just a leetle, leetle, tiny—thanks, thanks; you spoil me. But, as I was saying, Richard, or was about to say, my daughter has been allowed to rust; her aunt was a mere duenna; hence, in parenthesis, Richard, her distrust of me; my nature and that of the duenna are poles asunder—poles! But, now that I am here, now that I have given up the fight, and live henceforth for one only of my works—I have the modesty to say it is my best—my daughter—well, we shall put all that to rights. The neighbours, Richard?'

Dick was understood to say that there were many good families in the Vale of Thyme.

'You shall introduce us,' said the Admiral.

99

Dick's shirt was wet; he made a lumbering excuse to go; which Esther explained to herself by a fear of intrusion, and so set down to the merit side of Dick's account, while she proceeded to detain him.

'Before our walk?' she cried. 'Never! I must have my walk.'

'Let us all go,' said the Admiral, rising.

'You do not know that you are wanted,' she cried, leaning on his shoulder with a caress. 'I might wish to speak to my old friend about my new father. But you shall come to-day, you shall do all you want; I have set my heart on spoiling you.'

'I will just take one drop more,' said the Admiral, stooping to help himself to brandy. 'It is surprising how this journey has fatigued me. But I am growing old, I am growing old, I am growing old, and—I regret to add—bald.'

He cocked a white wide-awake coquettishly upon his head—the habit of the lady-killer clung to him; and Esther had already thrown on her hat, and was ready, while he was still studying the result in a mirror: the carbuncle had somewhat painfully arrested his attention.

'We are papa now; we must be respectable,' he said to Dick, in explanation of his dandyism: and then he went to a bundle and chose himself a staff. Where were the elegant canes of his Parisian epoch? This was a support for age, and designed for rustic scenes. Dick began to see and appreciate the man's enjoyment in a new part, when he saw how carefully he had 'made it up.' He had invented a gait for this first country stroll with his daughter, which was admirably in key. He walked with fatigue, he leaned upon the staff; he looked round him with a sad, smiling sympathy on all that he beheld; he even asked the name of a plant, and rallied himself gently for an old town bird, ignorant of nature. 'This country life will make me young again,' he sighed. They reached the top of the hill towards the first hour of evening; the sun was descending heaven, the colour had all drawn into the west; the hills were modelled in their least contour by the soft, slanting shine; and the wide moorlands, veined with glens and hazelwoods, ran west and north in a hazy glory of light. Then the painter wakened in Van Tromp.

'Gad, Dick,' he cried, 'what value!'

An ode in four hundred lines would not have seemed so touching to Esther; her eyes filled with happy tears; yes, here was the father of whom she had dreamed, whom Dick had described; simple, enthusiastic, unworldly, kind, a painter at heart, and a fine gentleman in manner.

And just then the Admiral perceived a house by the wayside, and something depending over the house door which might be construed as a sign by the hopeful and thirsty.

'Is that,' he asked, pointing with his stick, 'an inn?'

There was a marked change in his voice, as though he attached importance to the inquiry: Esther listened, hoping she should hear wit or wisdom.

Dick said it was.

'You know it?' inquired the Admiral.

'I have passed it a hundred times, but that is all,' replied Dick.

'Ah,' said Van Tromp, with a smile, and shaking his head; 'you are not an old campaigner; you have the world to learn. Now I, you see, find an inn so very near my own home, and my first thought is my neighbours. I shall go forward and make my neighbours' acquaintance; no, you needn't come; I shall not be a moment.'

And he walked off briskly towards the inn, leaving Dick alone with Esther on the road.

'Dick,' she exclaimed, 'I am so glad to get a word with you; I am so happy, I have such a thousand things to say; and I want you to do me a favour. Imagine, he has come without a paint-box, without an easel; and I want him to have all. I want you to get them for me in Thymebury. You saw, this moment, how his heart turned to painting. They can't live without it,' she added; meaning perhaps Van Tromp and Michel Angelo.

Up to that moment, she had observed nothing amiss in Dick's behaviour. She was too happy to be curious; and his silence, in presence of the great and good being whom she called her father, had seemed both natural and praiseworthy. But now that they were alone, she became conscious of a barrier between her lover and herself, and alarm sprang up in her heart.

101

'Dick,' she cried, 'you don't love me.'

'I do that,' he said heartily.

'But you are unhappy; you are strange; you—you are not glad to see my father,' she concluded, with a break in her voice.

'Esther,' he said, 'I tell you that I love you; if you love me, you know what that means, and that all I wish is to see you happy. Do you think I cannot enjoy your pleasures? Esther, I do. If I am uneasy, if I am alarmed, if—. Oh, believe me, try and believe in me,' he cried, giving up argument with perhaps a happy inspiration.

But the girl's suspicions were aroused; and though she pressed the matter no farther (indeed, her father was already seen returning), it by no means left her thoughts. At one moment she simply resented the selfishness of a man who had obtruded his dark looks and passionate language on her joy; for there is nothing that a woman can less easily forgive than the language of a passion which, even if only for the moment, she does not share. At another, she suspected him of jealousy against her father; and for that, although she could see excuses for it, she yet despised him. And at least, in one way or the other, here was the dangerous beginning of a separation between two hearts. Esther found herself at variance with her sweetest friend; she could no longer look into his heart and find it written with the same language as her own; she could no longer think of him as the sun which radiated happiness upon her life, for she had turned to him once, and he had breathed upon her black and chilly, radiated blackness and frost. To put the whole matter in a word, she was beginning, although ever so slightly, to fall out of love.

CHAPTER VI

THE PRODIGAL FATHER GOES ON FROM STRENGTH TO STRENGTH

We will not follow all the steps of the Admiral's return and installation, but hurry forward towards the catastrophe, merely chronicling by the way a few salient incidents, wherein we must rely entirely upon the evidence of Richard, for Esther to this day has never opened her mouth upon this trying passage of her life, and as for the Admiral—well, that naval officer, although still alive, and now more suitably installed in a seaport town where he has a telescope and a flag in his front garden, is incapable of throwing the slightest gleam of light upon the affair. Often and often has he remarked to the present writer: 'If I know what it was all about, sir, I'll be—' in short, be what I hope he will not. And then he will look across at his daughter's portrait, a photograph, shake his head with an amused appearance, and mix himself another grog by way of consolation. Once I heard him go farther, and express his feelings with regard to Esther in a single but eloquent word. 'A minx, sir,' he said, not in anger, rather in amusement: and he cordially drank her health upon the back of it. His worst enemy must admit him to be a man without malice; he never bore a grudge in his life, lacking the necessary taste and industry of attention.

Yet it was during this obscure period that the drama was really performed; and its scene was in the heart of Esther, shut away from all eyes. Had this warm, upright, sullen girl been differently used by destiny, had events come upon her even in a different succession, for some things lead easily to others, the whole course of this tale would have been changed, and Esther never would have run away. As it was, through a series of acts and words of which we know but few, and a series of thoughts which any one may imagine for himself, she was awakened in four days from the dream of a life.

The first tangible cause of disenchantment was when Dick brought home a painter's arsenal on Friday evening. The Admiral was in the chimney-corner, once more 'sirrupping' some brandy and water, and Esther sat at the table at work. They both came forward to greet the new arrival; and the girl, relieving him of his monstrous

103

burthen, proceeded to display her offerings to her father. Van Tromp's countenance fell several degrees; he became quite querulous.

'God bless me,' he said; and then, 'I must really ask you not to interfere, child,' in a tone of undisguised hostility.

'Father,' she said, 'forgive me; I knew you had given up your art—'

'Oh yes!' cried the Admiral; 'I've done with it to the judgment-day!'

'Pardon me again,' she said firmly, 'but I do not, I cannot think that you are right in this. Suppose the world is unjust, suppose that no one understands you, you have still a duty to yourself. And, oh, don't spoil the pleasure of your coming home to me; show me that you can be my father and yet not neglect your destiny. I am not like some daughters; I will not be jealous of your art, and I will try to understand it.'

The situation was odiously farcical. Richard groaned under it; he longed to leap forward and denounce the humbug. And the humbug himself? Do you fancy he was easier in his mind? I am sure, on the other hand, that he was acutely miserable; and he betrayed his sufferings by a perfectly silly and undignified access of temper, during which he broke his pipe in several pieces, threw his brandy and water in the fire, and employed words which were very plain although the drift of them was somewhat vague. It was of very brief duration. Van Tromp was himself again, and in a most delightful humour within three minutes of the first explosion.

'I am an old fool,' he said frankly. 'I was spoiled when a child. As for you, Esther, you take after your mother; you have a morbid sense of duty, particularly for others; strive against it, my dear— strive against it. And as for the pigments, well, I'll use them, some of these days; and to show that I'm in earnest, I'll get Dick here to prepare a canvas.'

Dick was put to this menial task forthwith, the Admiral not even watching how he did, but quite occupied with another grog and a pleasant vein of talk.

A little after Esther arose, and making some pretext, good or bad, went off to bed. Dick was left hobbled by the canvas, and was subjected to Van Tromp for about an hour.

The next day, Saturday, it is believed that little intercourse took place between Esther and her father; but towards the afternoon Dick met the latter returning from the direction of the inn, where he had struck up quite a friendship with the landlord. Dick wondered who paid for these excursions, and at the thought that the reprobate must get his pocket money where he got his board and lodging, from poor Esther's generosity, he had it almost in his heart to knock the old gentleman down. He, on his part, was full of airs and graces and geniality.

'Dear Dick,' he said, taking his arm, 'this is neighbourly of you; it shows your tact to meet me when I had a wish for you. I am in pleasant spirits; and it is then that I desire a friend.'

'I am glad to hear you are so happy,' retorted Dick bitterly. 'There's certainly not much to trouble you.'

'No,' assented the Admiral, 'not much. I got out of it in time; and here—well, here everything pleases me. I am plain in my tastes. 'A propos, you have never asked me how I liked my daughter?'

'No,' said Dick roundly; 'I certainly have not.'

'Meaning you will not. And why, Dick? She is my daughter, of course; but then I am a man of the world and a man of taste, and perfectly qualified to give an opinion with impartiality—yes, Dick, with impartiality. Frankly, I am not disappointed in her. She has good looks; she has them from her mother. So I may say I chose her looks. She is devoted, quite devoted to me—'

'She is the best woman in the world!' broke out Dick.

'Dick,' cried the Admiral, stopping short; 'I have been expecting this. Let us—let us go back to the "Trevanion Arms" and talk this matter out over a bottle.'

'Certainly not,' went Dick. 'You have had far too much already.'

The parasite was on the point of resenting this; but a look at Dick's face, and some recollection of the terms on which they had stood in Paris, came to the aid of his wisdom and restrained him.

'As you please,' he said; 'although I don't know what you mean—nor care. But let us walk, if you prefer it. You are still a young man; when you are my age— But, however, to continue. You please me, Dick; you have pleased me from the first; and to say truth, Esther is

105

a trifle fantastic, and will be better when she is married. She has means of her own, as of course you are aware. They come, like the looks, from her poor, dear, good creature of a mother. She was blessed in her mother. I mean she shall be blessed in her husband, and you are the man, Dick, you and not another. This very night I will sound her affections.'

Dick stood aghast.

'Mr. Van Tromp, I implore you,' he said; 'do what you please with yourself, but, for God's sake, let your daughter alone.'

'It is my duty,' replied the Admiral, 'and between ourselves, you rogue, my inclination too. I am as matchmaking as a dowager. It will be more discreet for you to stay away to-night. Farewell. You leave your case in good hands; I have the tact of these little matters by heart; it is not my first attempt.'

All arguments were in vain; the old rascal stuck to his point; nor did Richard conceal from himself how seriously this might injure his prospects, and he fought hard. Once there came a glimmer of hope. The Admiral again proposed an adjournment to the 'Trevanion Arms,' and when Dick had once more refused, it hung for a moment in the balance whether or not the old toper would return there by himself. Had he done so, of course Dick could have taken to his heels, and warned Esther of what was coming, and of how it had begun. But the Admiral, after a pause, decided for the brandy at home, and made off in that direction.

We have no details of the sounding.

Next day the Admiral was observed in the parish church, very properly dressed. He found the places, and joined in response and hymn, as to the manner born; and his appearance, as he intended it should, attracted some attention among the worshippers. Old Naseby, for instance, had observed him.

'There was a drunken-looking blackguard opposite us in church,' he said to his son as they drove home; 'do you know who he was?'

'Some fellow—Van Tromp, I believe,' said Dick.

'A foreigner, too!' observed the Squire.

Dick could not sufficiently congratulate himself on the escape he had effected. Had the Admiral met him with his father, what would have been the result? And could such a catastrophe be long postponed? It seemed to him as if the storm were nearly ripe; and it was so more nearly than he thought.

He did not go to the cottage in the afternoon, withheld by fear and shame; but when dinner was over at Naseby House, and the Squire had gone off into a comfortable doze, Dick slipped out of the room, and ran across country, in part to save time, in part to save his own courage from growing cold; for he now hated the notion of the cottage or the Admiral, and if he did not hate, at least feared to think of Esther. He had no clue to her reflections; but he could not conceal from his own heart that he must have sunk in her esteem, and the spectacle of her infatuation galled him like an insult.

He knocked and was admitted. The room looked very much as on his last visit, with Esther at the table and Van Tromp beside the fire; but the expression of the two faces told a very different story. The girl was paler than usual; her eyes were dark, the colour seemed to have faded from round about them, and her swiftest glance was as intent as a stare. The appearance of the Admiral, on the other hand, was rosy, and flabby, and moist; his jowl hung over his shirt collar, his smile was loose and wandering, and he had so far relaxed the natural control of his eyes, that one of them was aimed inward, as if to watch the growth of the carbuncle. We are warned against bad judgments; but the Admiral was certainly not sober. He made no attempt to rise when Richard entered, but waved his pipe flightily in the air, and gave a leer of welcome. Esther took as little notice of him as might be.

'Aha! Dick!' cried the painter. 'I've been to church; I have, upon my word. And I saw you there, though you didn't see me. And I saw a devilish pretty woman, by Gad. If it were not for this baldness, and a kind of crapulous air I can't disguise from myself—if it weren't for this and that and t'other thing—I—I've forgot what I was saying. Not that that matters, I've heaps of things to say. I'm in a communicative vein to-night. I'll let out all my cats, even unto seventy times seven. I'm in what I call the stage, and all I desire is a listener, although he were deaf, to be as happy as Nebuchadnezzar.'

Of the two hours which followed upon this it is unnecessary to give more than a sketch. The Admiral was extremely silly, now and then amusing, and never really offensive. It was plain that he kept in view the presence of his daughter, and chose subjects and a character of language that should not offend a lady. On almost any other occasion Dick would have enjoyed the scene. Van Tromp's egotism, flown with drink, struck a pitch above mere vanity. He became candid and explanatory; sought to take his auditors entirely into his confidence, and tell them his inmost conviction about himself. Between his self-knowledge, which was considerable, and his vanity, which was immense, he had created a strange hybrid animal, and called it by his own name. How he would plume his feathers over virtues which would have gladdened the heart of Cæsar or St. Paul; and anon, complete his own portrait with one of those touches of pitiless realism which the satirist so often seeks in vain.

'Now, there's Dick,' he said, 'he's shrewd; he saw through me the first time we met, and told me so—told me so to my face, which I had the virtue to keep. I bear you no malice for it, Dick; you were right; I am a humbug.'

You may fancy how Esther quailed at this new feature of the meeting between her two idols.

And then, again, in a parenthesis:—

'That,' said Van Tromp, 'was when I had to paint those dirty daubs of mine.'

And a little further on, laughingly said perhaps, but yet with an air of truth:—

'I never had the slightest hesitation in sponging upon any human creature.'

Thereupon Dick got up.

'I think perhaps,' he said, 'we had better all be thinking of going to bed.' And he smiled with a feeble and deprecatory smile.

'Not at all,' cried the Admiral, 'I know a trick worth two of that. Puss here,' indicating his daughter, 'shall go to bed; and you and I will keep it up till all's blue.'

Thereupon Esther arose in sullen glory. She had sat and listened for two mortal hours while her idol defiled himself and sneered away his godhead. One by one, her illusions had departed. And now he wished to order her to bed in her own house! now he called her Puss! now, even as he uttered the words, toppling on his chair, he broke the stem of his tobacco-pipe in three! Never did the sheep turn upon her shearer with a more commanding front. Her voice

108

was calm, her enunciation a little slow, but perfectly distinct, and she stood before him as she spoke, in the simplest and most maidenly attitude.

'No,' she said, 'Mr. Naseby will have the goodness to go home at once, and you will go to bed.'

The broken fragments of pipe fell from the Admiral's fingers; he seemed by his countenance to have lived too long in a world unworthy of him; but it is an odd circumstance, he attempted no reply, and sat thunderstruck, with open mouth.

Dick she motioned sharply towards the door, and he could only obey her. In the porch, finding she was close behind him, he ventured to pause and whisper, 'You have done right.'

'I have done as I pleased,' she said. 'Can he paint?'

'Many people like his paintings,' returned Dick, in stifled tones; 'I never did; I never said I did,' he added, fiercely defending himself before he was attacked.

'I ask you if he can paint. I will not be put off. Can he paint?' she repeated.

'No,' said Dick.

'Does he even like it?'

'Not now, I believe.'

'And he is drunk?'—she leaned upon the word with hatred.

'He has been drinking.'

'Go,' she said, and was turning to re-enter the house when another thought arrested her. 'Meet me to-morrow morning at the stile,' she said.

'I will,' replied Dick.

And then the door closed behind her, and Dick was alone in the darkness. There was still a chink of light above the sill, a warm, mild glow behind the window; the roof of the cottage and some of the banks and hazels were defined in denser darkness against the sky; but all else was formless, breathless, and noiseless like the pit.

Dick remained as she had left him, standing squarely upon one foot and resting only on the toe of the other, and as he stood he listened with his soul. The sound of a chair pushed sharply over the floor startled his heart into his mouth; but the silence which had thus been disturbed settled back again at once upon the cottage and its vicinity. What took place during this interval is a secret from the world of men; but when it was over the voice of Esther spoke evenly and without interruption for perhaps half a minute, and as soon as that ceased heavy and uncertain footfalls crossed the parlour and mounted lurching up the stairs. The girl had tamed her father, Van Tromp had gone obediently to bed: so much was obvious to the watcher in the road. And yet he still waited, straining his ears, and with terror and sickness at his heart; for if Esther had followed her father, if she had even made one movement in this great conspiracy of men and nature to be still, Dick must have had instant knowledge of it from his station before the door; and if she had not moved, must she not have fainted? or might she not be dead?

He could hear the cottage clock deliberately measure out the seconds; time stood still with him; an almost superstitious terror took command of his faculties; at last, he could bear no more, and, springing through the little garden in two bounds, he put his face against the window. The blind, which had not been drawn fully down, left an open chink about an inch in height along the bottom of the glass, and the whole parlour was thus exposed to Dick's investigation. Esther sat upright at the table, her head resting on her hand, her eyes fixed upon the candle. Her brows were slightly bent, her mouth slightly open; her whole attitude so still and settled that Dick could hardly fancy that she breathed. She had not stirred at the sound of Dick's arrival. Soon after, making a considerable disturbance amid the vast silence of the night, the clock lifted up its voice, whined for a while like a partridge, and then eleven times hooted like a cuckoo. Still Esther continued immovable and gazed upon the candle. Midnight followed, and then one of the morning; and still she had not stirred, nor had Richard Naseby dared to quit the window. And then, about half-past one, the candle she had been thus intently watching flared up into a last blaze of paper, and she leaped to her feet with an ejaculation, looked about her once, blew out the light, turned round, and was heard rapidly mounting the staircase in the dark.

Dick was left once more alone to darkness and to that dulled and dogged state of mind when a man thinks that Misery must now have done her worst, and is almost glad to think so. He turned and walked slowly towards the stile; she had told him no hour, and he was determined, whenever she came, that she should find him waiting. As he got there the day began to dawn, and he leaned over a hurdle and beheld the shadows flee away. Up went the sun at last out of a bank of clouds that were already disbanding in the east; a herald wind had already sprung up to sweep the leafy earth and scatter the congregated dewdrops. 'Alas!' thought Dick Naseby, 'how can any other day come so distastefully to me?' He still wanted his experience of the morrow.

CHAPTER VII
THE ELOPEMENT

It was probably on the stroke of ten, and Dick had been half asleep for some time against the bank, when Esther came up the road carrying a bundle. Some kind of instinct, or perhaps the distant light footfalls, recalled him, while she was still a good way off, to the possession of his faculties, and he half raised himself and blinked upon the world. It took him some time to recollect his thoughts. He had awakened with a certain blank and childish sense of pleasure, like a man who had received a legacy overnight; but this feeling gradually died away, and was then suddenly and stunningly succeeded by a conviction of the truth. The whole story of the past night sprang into his mind with every detail, as by an exercise of the direct and speedy sense of sight, and he arose from the ditch and, with rueful courage, went to meet his love.

She came up to him walking steady and fast, her face still pale, but to all appearance perfectly composed; and she showed neither surprise, relief, nor pleasure at finding her lover on the spot. Nor did she offer him her hand.

'Here I am,' said he.

'Yes,' she replied; and then, without a pause or any change of voice, 'I want you to take me away,' she added.

'Away?' he repeated. 'How? Where?'

'To-day,' she said. 'I do not care where it is, but I want you to take me away.'

'For how long? I do not understand,' gasped Dick.

'I shall never come back here any more,' was all she answered.

Wild words uttered, as these were, with perfect quiet of manner and voice, exercise a double influence on the hearer's mind. Dick was confounded; he recovered from astonishment only to fall into doubt and alarm. He looked upon her frozen attitude, so discouraging for a lover to behold, and recoiled from the thoughts which it suggested.

'To me?' he asked. 'Are you coming to me, Esther?'

'I want you to take me away,' she repeated with weary impatience. 'Take me away—take me away from here.'

The situation was not sufficiently defined. Dick asked himself with concern whether she were altogether in her right wits. To take her away, to marry her, to work off his hands for her support, Dick was content to do all this; yet he required some show of love upon her part. He was not one of those tough-hided and small-hearted males who would marry their love at the point of the bayonet rather than not marry her at all. He desired that a woman should come to his arms with an attractive willingness, if not with ardour. And Esther's bearing was more that of despair than that of love. It chilled him and taught him wisdom.

'Dearest,' he urged, 'tell me what you wish, and you shall have it; tell me your thoughts, and then I can advise you. But to go from here without a plan, without forethought, in the heat of a moment, is madder than madness, and can help nothing. I am not speaking like a man, but I speak the truth; and I tell you again, the thing's absurd, and wrong, and hurtful.'

She looked at him with a lowering, languid look of wrath.

'So you will not take me?' she said. 'Well, I will go alone.'

And she began to step forward on her way. But he threw himself before her.

'Esther, Esther!' he cried.

'Let me go—don't touch me—what right have you to interfere? Who are you, to touch me?' she flashed out, shrill with anger.

Then, being made bold by her violence, he took her firmly, almost roughly, by the arm, and held her while he spoke.

'You know well who I am, and what I am, and that I love you. You say I will not help you; but your heart knows the contrary. It is you who will not help me; for you will not tell me what you want. You see—or you could see, if you took the pains to look—how I have waited here all night to be ready at your service. I only asked information; I only urged you to consider; and I still urge and beg you to think better of your fancies. But if your mind is made up, so be it; I will beg no longer; I give you my orders; and I will not allow—not allow you to go hence alone.'

She looked at him for awhile with cold, unkind scrutiny like one who tries the temper of a tool.

'Well, take me away, then,' she said with a sigh.

'Good,' said Dick. 'Come with me to the stables; there we shall get the pony-trap and drive to the junction. To-night you shall be in London. I am yours so wholly that no words can make me more so; and, besides, you know it, and the words are needless. May God help me to be good to you, Esther—may God help me! for I see that you will not.'

So, without more speech, they set out together, and were already got some distance from the spot, ere he observed that she was still carrying the hand-bag. She gave it up to him, passively, but when he offered her his arm, merely shook her head and pursed up her lips. The sun shone clearly and pleasantly; the wind was fresh and brisk upon their faces, and smelt racily of woods and meadows. As they went down into the valley of the Thyme, the babble of the stream rose into the air like a perennial laughter. On the far-away hills, sun-burst and shadow raced along the slopes and leaped from peak to peak. Earth, air and water, each seemed in better health and had more of the shrewd salt of life in them than upon ordinary mornings; and from east to west, from the lowest glen to the height of heaven, from every look and touch and scent, a human creature could gather the most encouraging intelligence as to the durability and spirit of the universe.

Through all this walked Esther, picking her small steps like a bird, but silent and with a cloud under her thick eyebrows. She seemed insensible, not only of nature, but of the presence of her companion. She was altogether engrossed in herself, and looked neither to right nor to left, but straight before her on the road. When they came to the bridge, however, she halted, leaned on the parapet, and stared for a moment at the clear, brown pool, and swift, transient snowdrift of the rapids.

'I am going to drink,' she said; and descended the winding footpath to the margin.

114

There she drank greedily in her hands and washed her temples with water. The coolness seemed to break, for an instant, the spell that lay upon her; for, instead of hastening forward again in her dull, indefatigable tramp, she stood still where she was, for near a minute, looking straight before her. And Dick, from above on the bridge where he stood to watch her, saw a strange, equivocal smile dawn slowly on her face and pass away again at once and suddenly, leaving her as grave as ever; and the sense of distance, which it is so cruel for a lover to endure, pressed with every moment more heavily on her companion. Her thoughts were all secret; her heart was locked and bolted; and he stood without, vainly wooing her with his eyes.

'Do you feel better?' asked Dick, as she at last rejoined him; and after the constraint of so long a silence, his voice sounded foreign to his own ears.

She looked at him for an appreciable fraction of a minute ere she answered, and when she did, it was in the monosyllable—'Yes.'

Dick's solicitude was nipped and frosted. His words died away on his tongue. Even his eyes, despairing of encouragement, ceased to attend on hers. And they went on in silence through Kirton hamlet, where an old man followed them with his eyes, and perhaps envied them their youth and love; and across the Ivy beck where the mill was splashing and grumbling low thunder to itself in the chequered shadow of the dell, and the miller before the door was beating flour from his hands as he whistled a modulation; and up by the high spinney, whence they saw the mountains upon either hand; and down the hill again to the back courts and offices of Naseby House. Esther had kept ahead all the way, and Dick plodded obediently in her wake; but as they neared the stables, he pushed on and took the lead. He would have preferred her to await him in the road while he went on and brought the carriage back, but after so many repulses and rebuffs he lacked courage to offer the suggestion. Perhaps, too, he felt it wiser to keep his convoy within sight. So they entered the yard in Indian file, like a tramp and his wife.

The grooms eyebrows rose as he received the order for the pony-phaeton, and kept rising during all his preparations. Esther stood bolt upright and looked steadily at some chickens in the corner of the yard. Master Richard himself, thought the groom, was not in his ordinary; for in truth, he carried the hand-bag like a talisman, and either stood listless, or set off suddenly walking in one direction after another with brisk, decisive footsteps. Moreover he had

115

apparently neglected to wash his hands, and bore the air of one returning from a prolonged nutting ramble. Upon the groom's countenance there began to grow up an expression as of one about to whistle. And hardly had the carriage turned the corner and rattled into the high road with this inexplicable pair, than the whistle broke forth—prolonged, and low and tremulous; and the groom, already so far relieved, vented the rest of his surprise in one simple English word, friendly to the mouth of Jack-tar and the sooty pitman, and hurried to spread the news round the servants' hall of Naseby House. Luncheon would be on the table in little beyond an hour; and the Squire, on sitting down, would hardly fail to ask for Master Richard. Hence, as the intelligent reader can foresee, this groom has a part to play in the imbroglio.

Meantime, Dick had been thinking deeply and bitterly. It seemed to him as if his love had gone from him, indeed, yet gone but a little way; as if he needed but to find the right touch or intonation, and her heart would recognise him and be melted. Yet he durst not open his mouth, and drove in silence till they had passed the main park-gates and turned into the cross-cut lane along the wall. Then it seemed to him as if it must be now, or never.

'Can't you see you are killing me?' he cried. 'Speak to me, look at me, treat me like a human man.'

She turned slowly and looked him in the face with eyes that seemed kinder. He dropped the reins and caught her hand, and she made no resistance, although her touch was unresponsive. But when, throwing one arm round her waist, he sought to kiss her lips, not like a lover indeed, not because he wanted to do so, but as a desperate man who puts his fortunes to the touch, she drew away from him, with a knot in her forehead, backed and shied about fiercely with her head, and pushed him from her with her hand. Then there was no room left for doubt, and Dick saw, as clear as sunlight, that she had a distaste or nourished a grudge against him.

'Then you don't love me?' he said, drawing back from her, he also, as though her touch had burnt him; and then, as she made no answer, he repeated with another intonation, imperious and yet still pathetic, 'You don't love me, do you, do you?'

'I don't know,' she replied. 'Why do you ask me? Oh, how should I know? It has all been lies together—lies, and lies, and lies!'

He cried her name sharply, like a man who has taken a physical

116

hurt, and that was the last word that either of them spoke until they reached Thymebury Junction.

This was a station isolated in the midst of moorlands, yet lying on the great up line to London. The nearest town, Thymebury itself, was seven miles distant along the branch they call the Vale of Thyme Railway. It was now nearly half an hour past noon, the down train had just gone by, and there would be no more traffic at the junction until half-past three, when the local train comes in to meet the up express at a quarter before four. The stationmaster had already gone off to his garden, which was half a mile away in a hollow of the moor; a porter, who was just leaving, took charge of the phaeton, and promised to return it before night to Naseby House; only a deaf, snuffy, and stern old man remained to play propriety for Dick and Esther.

Before the phaeton had driven off, the girl had entered the station and seated herself upon a bench. The endless, empty moorlands stretched before her, entirely unenclosed, and with no boundary but the horizon. Two lines of rails, a waggon shed, and a few telegraph posts, alone diversified the outlook. As for sounds, the silence was unbroken save by the chant of the telegraph wires and the crying of the plovers on the waste. With the approach of midday the wind had more and more fallen, it was now sweltering hot and the air trembled in the sunshine.

Dick paused for an instant on the threshold of the platform. Then, in two steps, he was by her side and speaking almost with a sob.

'Esther,' he said, 'have pity on me. What have I done? Can you not forgive me? Esther, you loved me once—can you not love me still?'

'How can I tell you? How am I to know?' she answered. 'You are all a lie to me—all a lie from first to last. You were laughing at my folly, playing with me like a child, at the very time when you declared you loved me. Which was true? was any of it true? or was it all, all a mockery? I am weary trying to find out. And you say I loved you; I loved my father's friend. I never loved, I never heard of, you, until that man came home and I began to find myself deceived. Give me back my father, be what you were before, and you may talk of love indeed!'

'Then you cannot forgive me—cannot?' he asked.

'I have nothing to forgive,' she answered. 'You do not understand.'

117

'Is that your last word, Esther?' said he, very white, and biting his lip to keep it still.

'Yes, that is my last word,' replied she.

'Then we are here on false pretences, and we stay here no longer,' he said. 'Had you still loved me, right or wrong, I should have taken you away, because then I could have made you happy. But as it is—I must speak plainly—what you propose is degrading to you, and an insult to me, and a rank unkindness to your father. Your father may be this or that, but you should use him like a fellow-creature.'

'What do you mean?' she flashed. 'I leave him my house and all my money; it is more than he deserves. I wonder you dare speak to me about that man. And besides, it is all he cares for; let him take it, and let me never hear from him again.'

'I thought you romantic about fathers,' he said.

'Is that a taunt?' she demanded.

'No,' he replied, 'it is an argument. No one can make you like him, but don't disgrace him in his own eyes. He is old, Esther, old and broken down. Even I am sorry for him, and he has been the loss of all I cared for. Write to your aunt; when I see her answer you can leave quietly and naturally, and I will take you to your aunt's door. But in the meantime you must go home. You have no money, and so you are helpless, and must do as I tell you; and believe me, Esther, I do all for your good, and your good only, so God help me.'

She had put her hand into her pocket and withdrawn it empty.

'I counted upon you,' she wailed.

'You counted rightly then,' he retorted. 'I will not, to please you for a moment, make both of us unhappy for our lives; and since I cannot marry you, we have only been too long away, and must go home at once.'

'Dick,' she cried suddenly, 'perhaps I might—perhaps in time—perhaps—'

'There is no perhaps about the matter,' interrupted Dick. 'I must go and bring the phaeton.' And with that he strode from the station, all in a glow of passion and virtue. Esther, whose eyes had come alive and her cheeks flushed during these last words, relapsed in a second

118

into a state of petrifaction. She remained without motion during his absence, and when he returned suffered herself to be put back into the phaeton, and driven off on the return journey like an idiot or a tired child. Compared with what she was now, her condition of the morning seemed positively natural. She sat white and cold and silent, and there was no speculation in her eyes. Poor Dick flailed and flailed at the pony, and once tried to whistle, but his courage was going down; huge clouds of despair gathered together in his soul, and from time to time their darkness was divided by a piercing flash of longing and regret. He had lost his love—he had lost his love for good.

The pony was tired, and the hills very long and steep, and the air sultrier than ever, for now the breeze began to fail entirely. It seemed as if this miserable drive would never be done, as if poor Dick would never be able to go away and be comfortably wretched by himself; for all his desire was to escape from her presence and the reproach of her averted looks. He had lost his love, he thought— he had lost his love for good.

They were already not far from the cottage, when his heart again faltered and he appealed to her once more, speaking low and eagerly in broken phrases.

'I cannot live without your love,' he concluded.

'I do not understand what you mean,' she replied, and I believe with perfect truth.

'Then,' said he, wounded to the quick, 'your aunt might come and fetch you herself. Of course you can command me as you please. But I think it would be better so.'

'Oh yes,' she said wearily, 'better so.'

This was the only exchange of words between them till about four o'clock; the phaeton, mounting the lane, 'opened out' the cottage between the leafy banks. Thin smoke went straight up from the chimney; the flowers in the garden, the hawthorn in the lane, hung down their heads in the heat; the stillness was broken only by the sound of hoofs. For right before the gate a livery servant rode slowly up and down, leading a saddle horse. And in this last Dick shuddered to identify his father's chestnut.

Alas! poor Richard, what should this portend?

119

The servant, as in duty bound, dismounted and took the phaeton into his keeping; yet Dick thought he touched his hat to him with something of a grin. Esther, passive as ever, was helped out and crossed the garden with a slow and mechanical gait; and Dick, following close behind her, heard from within the cottage his father's voice upraised in an anathema, and the shriller tones of the Admiral responding in the key of war.

CHAPTER VIII

BATTLE ROYAL

Squire Naseby, on sitting down to lunch, had inquired for Dick, whom he had not seen since the day before at dinner; and the servant answering awkwardly that Master Richard had come back but had gone out again with the pony phaeton, his suspicions became aroused, and he cross-questioned the man until the whole was out. It appeared from this report that Dick had been going about for nearly a month with a girl in the Vale—a Miss Van Tromp; that she lived near Lord Trevanion's upper wood; that recently Miss Van Tromp's papa had returned home from foreign parts after a prolonged absence; that this papa was an old gentleman, very chatty and free with his money in the public-house—whereupon Mr. Naseby's face became encrimsoned; that the papa, furthermore, was said to be an admiral—whereupon Mr. Naseby spat out a whistle brief and fierce as an oath; that Master Dick seemed very friendly with the papa—'God help him!' said Mr. Naseby; that last night Master Dick had not come in, and to-day he had driven away in the phaeton with the young lady—

'Young woman,' corrected Mr. Naseby.

'Yes, sir,' said the man, who had been unwilling enough to gossip from the first, and was now cowed by the effect of his communications on the master. 'Young woman, sir!'

'Had they luggage?' demanded the Squire.

'Yes, sir.'

Mr. Naseby was silent for a moment, struggling to keep down his emotion, and he mastered it so far as to mount into the sarcastic vein, when he was in the nearest danger of melting into the sorrowful.

'And was this—this Van Dunk with them?' he asked, dwelling scornfully upon the name.

The servant believed not, and being eager to shift the responsibility

121

of speech to other shoulders, suggested that perhaps the master had better inquire further from George the stableman in person.

'Tell him to saddle the chestnut and come with me. He can take the gray gelding; for we may ride fast. And then you can take away this trash,' added Mr. Naseby, pointing to the luncheon; and he arose, lordly in his anger, and marched forth upon the terrace to await his horse.

There Dick's old nurse shrunk up to him, for the news went like wildfire over Naseby House, and timidly expressed a hope that there was nothing much amiss with the young master.

'I'll pull him through,' the Squire said grimly, as though he meant to pull him through a threshing-mill; 'I'll save him from this gang; God help him with the next! He has a taste for low company, and no natural affections to steady him. His father was no society for him; he must go fuddling with a Dutchman, Nance, and now he's caught. Let us pray he'll take the lesson,' he added more gravely, 'but youth is here to make troubles, and age to pull them out again.'

Nance whimpered and recalled several episodes of Dick's childhood, which moved Mr. Naseby to blow his nose and shake her hard by the hand; and then, the horse arriving opportunely, to get himself without delay into the saddle and canter off.

He rode straight, hot spur, to Thymebury, where, as was to be expected, he could glean no tidings of the runaways. They had not been seen at the George; they had not been seen at the station. The shadow darkened on Mr. Naseby's face; the junction did not occur to him; his last hope was for Van Tromp's cottage; thither he bade George guide him, and thither he followed, nursing grief, anxiety, and indignation in his heart.

'Here it is, sir,' said George stopping.

'What! on my own land!' he cried. 'How's this? I let this place to somebody—M'Whirter or M'Glashan.'

'Miss M'Glashan was the young lady's aunt, sir, I believe,' returned George.

'Ay—dummies,' said the Squire. 'I shall whistle for my rent too. Here, take my horse.'

The Admiral, this hot afternoon, was sitting by the window with a

122

long glass. He already knew the Squire by sight, and now, seeing him dismount before the cottage and come striding through the garden, concluded without doubt he was there to ask for Esther's hand.

'This is why the girl is not yet home,' he thought: 'a very suitable delicacy on young Naseby's part.'

And he composed himself with some pomp, answered the loud rattle of the riding-whip upon the door with a dulcet invitation to enter, and coming forward with a bow and a smile, 'Mr. Naseby, I believe,' said he.

The Squire came armed for battle; took in his man from top to toe in one rapid and scornful glance, and decided on a course at once. He must let the fellow see that he understood him.

'You are Mr. Van Tromp?' he returned roughly, and without taking any notice of the proffered hand.

'The same, sir,' replied the Admiral. 'Pray be seated.'

'No sir,' said the Squire, point-blank, 'I will not be seated. I am told that you are an admiral,' he added.

'No sir, I am not an admiral,' returned Van Tromp, who now began to grow nettled and enter into the spirit of the interview.

'Then why do you call yourself one, sir?'

'I have to ask your pardon, I do not,' says Van Tromp, as grand as the Pope.

But nothing was of avail against the Squire.

'You sail under false colours from beginning to end,' he said. 'Your very house was taken under a sham name.'

'It is not my house. I am my daughter's guest,' replied the Admiral. 'If it were my house—'

'Well?' said the Squire, 'what then? hey?'

The Admiral looked at him nobly, but was silent.

'Look here,' said Mr. Naseby, 'this intimidation is a waste of time; it is thrown away on me, sir; it will not succeed with me. I will not permit you even to gain time by your fencing. Now, sir, I presume you understand what brings me here.'

'I am entirely at a loss to account for your intrusion,' bows and waves Van Tromp.

'I will try to tell you then. I come here as a father'—down came the riding-whip upon the table—'I have right and justice upon my side. I understand your calculations, but you calculated without me. I am a man of the world, and I see through you and your manœuvres. I am dealing now with a conspiracy—I stigmatise it as such, and I will expose it and crush it. And now I order you to tell me how far things have gone, and whither you have smuggled my unhappy son.'

'My God, sir!' Van Tromp broke out, 'I have had about enough of this. Your son? God knows where he is for me! What the devil have I to do with your son? My daughter is out, for the matter of that; I might ask you where she was, and what would you say to that? But this is all midsummer madness. Name your business distinctly, and be off.'

'How often am I to tell you?' cried the Squire. 'Where did your daughter take my son to-day in that cursed pony carriage?'

'In a pony carriage?' repeated Van Tromp.

'Yes, sir—with luggage.'

'Luggage?'—Van Tromp had turned a little pale.

'Luggage, I said—luggage!' shouted Naseby. 'You may spare me this dissimulation. Where's my son. You are speaking to a father, sir, a father.'

'But, sir, if this be true,' out came Van Tromp in a new key, 'it is I who have an explanation to demand?'

'Precisely. There is the conspiracy,' retorted Naseby. 'Oh!' he added, 'I am a man of the world. I can see through and through you.'

Van Tromp began to understand.

'You speak a great deal about being a father, Mr. Naseby,' said he; 'I believe you forget that the appellation is common to both of us. I am at a loss to figure to myself, however dimly, how any man—I have not said any gentleman—could so brazenly insult another as you have been insulting me since you entered this house. For the first time I appreciate your base insinuations, and I despise them and you. You were, I am told, a manufacturer; I am an artist; I have seen better days; I have moved in societies where you would not be received, and dined where you would be glad to pay a pound to see me dining. The so-called aristocracy of wealth, sir, I despise. I refuse to help you; I refuse to be helped by you. There lies the door.'

And the Admiral stood forth in a halo.

It was then that Dick entered. He had been waiting in the porch for some time back, and Esther had been listlessly standing by his side. He had put out his hand to bar her entrance, and she had submitted without surprise; and though she seemed to listen, she scarcely appeared to comprehend. Dick, on his part, was as white as a sheet; his eyes burned and his lips trembled with anger as he thrust the door suddenly open, introduced Esther with ceremonious gallantry, and stood forward and knocked his hat firmer on his head like a man about to leap.

'What is all this?' he demanded.

'Is this your father, Mr. Naseby?' inquired the Admiral.

'It is,' said the young man.

'I make you my compliments,' returned Van Tromp.

'Dick!' cried his father, suddenly breaking forth, 'it is not too late, is it? I have come here in time to save you. Come, come away with me—come away from this place.'

And he fawned upon Dick with his hands.

'Keep your hands off me,' cried Dick, not meaning unkindness, but because his nerves were shattered by so many successive miseries.

'No, no,' said the old man, 'don't repulse your father, Dick, when he has come here to save you. Don't repulse me, my boy. Perhaps I have not been kind to you, not quite considerate, too harsh; my boy, it was not for want of love. Think of old times. I was kind to you then, was I not? When you were a child, and your mother was with us.' Mr. Naseby was interrupted by a sort of sob. Dick stood looking at him in a maze. 'Come away,' pursued the father in a whisper; 'you need not be afraid of any consequences. I am a man

125

of the world, Dick; and she can have no claim on you—no claim, I tell you; and we'll be handsome too, Dick—we'll give them a good round figure, father and daughter, and there's an end.'

He had been trying to get Dick towards the door, but the latter stood off.

'You had better take care, sir, how you insult that lady,' said the son, as black as night.

'You would not choose between your father and your mistress?' said the father.

'What do you call her, sir?' cried Dick, high and clear.

Forbearance and patience were not among Mr. Naseby's qualities.

'I called her your mistress,' he shouted, 'and I might have called her a—'

'That is an unmanly lie,' replied Dick, slowly.

'Dick!' cried the father, 'Dick!'

'I do not care,' said the son, strengthening himself against his own heart; 'I—I have said it, and it is the truth.'

There was a pause.

'Dick,' said the old man at last, in a voice that was shaken as by a gale of wind, 'I am going. I leave you with your friends, sir—with your friends. I came to serve you, and now I go away a broken man. For years I have seen this coming, and now it has come. You never loved me. Now you have been the death of me. You may boast of that. Now I leave you. God pardon you.'

With that he was gone; and the three who remained together heard his horse's hoofs descend the lane. Esther had not made a sign throughout the interview, and still kept silence now that it was over; but the Admiral, who had once or twice moved forward and drawn back again, now advanced for good.

'You are a man of spirit, sir,' said he to Dick; 'but though I am no friend to parental interference, I will say that you were heavy on the governor.' Then he added with a chuckle: 'You began, Richard, with a silver spoon, and here you are in the water like the rest. Work,

work, nothing like work. You have parts, you have manners; why, with application you may die a millionaire!' Dick shook himself. He took Esther by the hand, looking at her mournfully.

'Then this is farewell,' he said.

'Yes,' she answered. There was no tone in her voice, and she did not return his gaze.

'For ever,' added Dick.

'For ever,' she repeated mechanically.

'I have had hard measure,' he continued. 'In time I believe I could have shown you I was worthy, and there was no time long enough to show how much I loved you. But it was not to be. I have lost all.'

He relinquished her hand, still looking at her, and she turned to leave the room.

'Why, what in fortune's name is the meaning of all this?' cried Van Tromp. 'Esther come back!'

'Let her go,' said Dick, and he watched her disappear with strangely mingled feelings. For he had fallen into that stage when men have the vertigo of misfortune, court the strokes of destiny, and rush towards anything decisive, that it may free them from suspense though at the cost of ruin. It is one of the many minor forms of suicide.

'She did not love me,' he said, turning to her father.

'I feared as much,' said he, 'when I sounded her. Poor Dick, poor Dick. And yet I believe I am as much cut up as you are. I was born to see others happy.'

'You forget,' returned Dick, with something like a sneer, 'that I am now a pauper.'

Van Tromp snapped his fingers.

'Tut!' said he; 'Esther has plenty for us all.'

Dick looked at him with some wonder. It had never dawned upon him that this shiftless, thriftless, worthless, sponging parasite was yet, after and in spite of all, not mercenary in the issue of his thoughts; yet so it was.

127

'Now,' said Dick, 'I must go.'

'Go?' cried Van Tromp. 'Where? Not one foot, Mr. Richard Naseby. Here you shall stay in the meantime! and—well, and do something practical—advertise for a situation as private secretary—and when you have it, go and welcome. But in the meantime, sir, no false pride; we must stay with our friends; we must sponge a while on Papa Van Tromp, who has sponged so often upon us.'

'By God,' cried Dick, 'I believe you are the best of the lot.'

'Dick, my boy,' replied the Admiral, winking, 'you mark me, I am not the worst.'

'Then why,' began Dick, and then paused. 'But Esther,' he began again, once more to interrupt himself. 'The fact is, Admiral,' he came out with it roundly now, 'your daughter wished to run away from you to-day, and I only brought her back with difficulty.'

'In the pony carriage?' asked the Admiral, with the silliness of extreme surprise.

'Yes,' Dick answered.

'Why, what the devil was she running away from?'

Dick found the question unusually hard to answer.

'Why,' said he, 'you know, you're a bit of a rip.'

'I behave to that girl, sir, like an archdeacon,' replied Van Tromp warmly.

'Well—excuse me—but you know you drink,' insisted Dick.

'I know that I was a sheet in the wind's eye, sir, once—once only, since I reached this place,' retorted the Admiral. 'And even then I was fit for any drawing-room. I should like you to tell me how many fathers, lay and clerical, go upstairs every day with a face like a lobster and cod's eyes—and are dull, upon the back of it—not even mirth for the money! No, if that's what she runs for, all I say is, let her run.'

'You see,' Dick tried it again, 'she has fancies—'

'Confound her fancies!' cried Van Tromp. 'I used her kindly; she had her own way; I was her father. Besides I had taken quite a liking to the girl, and meant to stay with her for good. But I tell you what it is, Dick, since she has trifled with you—Oh, yes, she did though!—and since her old papa's not good enough for her—the devil take her, say I.'

'You will be kind to her at least?' said Dick.

'I never was unkind to a living soul,' replied the Admiral. 'Firm I can be, but not unkind.'

'Well,' said Dick, offering his hand, 'God bless you, and farewell.'

The Admiral swore by all his gods he should not go. 'Dick,' he said, 'You are a selfish dog; you forget your old Admiral. You wouldn't leave him alone, would you?'

It was useless to remind him that the house was not his to dispose of, that being a class of considerations to which his intelligence was closed; so Dick tore himself off by force, and, shouting a good-bye, made off along the lane to Thymebury.

CHAPTER IX

IN WHICH THE LIBERAL EDITOR RE-APPEARS AS 'DEUS EX MACHINA'

It was perhaps a week later, as old Mr. Naseby sat brooding in his study, that there was shown in upon him, on urgent business, a little hectic gentleman shabbily attired.

'I have to ask pardon for this intrusion, Mr. Naseby,' he said; 'but I come here to perform a duty. My card has been sent in, but perhaps you may not know, what it does not tell you, that I am the editor of the Thymebury Star.'

Mr. Naseby looked up, indignant.

'I cannot fancy,' he said, 'that we have much in common to discuss.'

'I have only a word to say—one piece of information to communicate. Some months ago, we had—you will pardon my referring to it, it is absolutely necessary—but we had an unfortunate difference as to facts.'

'Have you come to apologise?' asked the Squire, sternly.

'No, sir; to mention a circumstance. On the morning in question, your son, Mr. Richard Naseby—'

'I do not permit his name to be mentioned.'

'You will, however, permit me,' replied the Editor.

'You are cruel,' said the Squire. He was right, he was a broken man.

Then the Editor described Dick's warning visit; and how he had seen in the lad's eye that there was a thrashing in the wind, and had escaped through pity only—so the Editor put it—'through pity only sir. And oh, sir,' he went on, 'if you had seen him speaking up for you, I am sure you would have been proud of your son. I know I admired the lad myself, and indeed that's what brings me here.'

'I have misjudged him,' said the Squire. 'Do you know where he is?'

130

'Yes, sir, he lies sick at Thymebury.'

'You can take me to him?'

'I can.'

'I pray God he may forgive me,' said the father.

And he and the Editor made post-haste for the country town.

Next day the report went abroad that Mr. Richard was reconciled to his father and had been taken home to Naseby House. He was still ailing, it was said, and the Squire nursed him like the proverbial woman. Rumour, in this instance, did no more than justice to the truth; and over the sickbed many confidences were exchanged, and clouds that had been growing for years passed away in a few hours, and as fond mankind loves to hope, for ever. Many long talks had been fruitless in external action, though fruitful for the understanding of the pair; but at last, one showery Tuesday, the Squire might have been observed upon his way to the cottage in the lane.

The old gentleman had arranged his features with a view to self-command, rather than external cheerfulness; and he entered the cottage on his visit of conciliation with the bearing of a clergyman come to announce a death.

The Admiral and his daughter were both within, and both looked upon their visitor with more surprise than favour.

'Sir,' said he to Van Tromp, 'I am told I have done you much injustice.'

There came a little sound in Esther's throat, and she put her hand suddenly to her heart.

'You have, sir; and the acknowledgment suffices,' replied the Admiral. 'I am prepared, sir, to be easy with you, since I hear you have made it up with my friend Dick. But let me remind you that you owe some apologies to this young lady also.'

'I shall have the temerity to ask for more than her forgiveness,' said the Squire. 'Miss Van Tromp,' he continued, 'once I was in great distress, and knew nothing of you or your character; but I believe you will pardon a few rough words to an old man who asks forgiveness from his heart. I have heard much of you since then; for

131

you have a fervent advocate in my house. I believe you will understand that I speak of my son. He is, I regret to say, very far from well; he does not pick up as the doctors had expected; he has a great deal upon his mind, and, to tell you the truth, my girl, if you won't help us, I am afraid I shall lose him. Come now, forgive him! I was angry with him once myself, and I found I was in the wrong. This is only a misunderstanding, like the other, believe me; and with one kind movement, you may give happiness to him, and to me, and to yourself.'

Esther made a movement towards the door, but long before she reached it she had broken forth sobbing.

'It is all right,' said the Admiral; 'I understand the sex. Let me make you my compliments, Mr. Naseby.'

The Squire was too much relieved to be angry.

'My dear,' said he to Esther, 'you must not agitate yourself.'

'She had better go up and see him right away,' suggested Van Tromp.

'I had not ventured to propose it,' replied the Squire. 'Les convenances, I believe—'

'Je m'en fiche,' cried the Admiral, snapping his fingers. 'She shall go and see my friend Dick. Run and get ready, Esther.'

Esther obeyed.

'She has not—has not run away again?' inquired Mr. Naseby, as soon as she was gone.

'No,' said Van Tromp, 'not again. She is a devilish odd girl though, mind you that.'

'But I cannot stomach the man with the carbuncles,' thought the Squire.

And this is why there is a new household and a brand-new baby in Naseby Dower House; and why the great Van Tromp lives in pleasant style upon the shores of England; and why twenty-six individual copies of the Thymebury Star are received daily at the door of Naseby House.

www.ingramcontent.com/pod-product-compliance
Lightning Source LLC
Chambersburg PA
CBHW011514170626
46810CB00009B/3364